I0659224

a companion novel to *Him* and *Her*

sawyer says

New York Times Bestselling Author
Carey Heywood

Sawyer Says

Copyright 2013 by Carey Heywood

ISBN: 978-0-9914362-3-1

All rights reserved. Except as permitted under the U.S. Copyright Act of 1976, no part of this publication may be reproduced, distributed, or transmitted in any form or by any means, or stored in a database or retrieval system, without prior written permission of the author.

The scanning, uploading, and distribution of this book via the Internet or via other means without the permission of the publisher is illegal and the punishable by law. Please purchase only authorized electronic editions and do not participate in or encourage electronic piracy of copyrighted materials. Your support of the author's rights is appreciated.

Sawyer Says is a work of fiction. Names, characters, places, and incidents are either the product of the author's imagination or are used fictitiously. Any resemblance to actual persons, living or dead, events, or locales is entirely coincidental.

dedication

*To my readers, you fell in love with Sawyer in Him & Her
and asked for her story. This book is for you.*

prologue

Her eyes blink open in an unfamiliar room.

"Mommy?" A whispered plea escapes her lips and echoes in the dark room.

"Daddy?" It's more a sob now that she's truly awake and remembers they're gone.

She curls into herself. Her arms wrap around her knees, and her knees press to her chest. Silent tears fall onto her pillow, the dampening fabric cool against her cheek.

There will be no more gentle fingers pulling back her mop of blonde hair to give her good morning kisses. There will be no more following her daddy around like his shadow until he scoops her up and carries her piggyback.

A creak from the hallway silences her. She is awake. Her grandmother. Last night when Sawyer had tried to hug her, she tsked, telling her it was late and they both needed their rest.

Tears, not lullabies, had been her company as exhaustion coaxed her to sleep. Everything was happening so fast. She had wanted to stay with Beau and Bess. Why did they let that lady take her? Then she was riding on a plane all alone to New Hampshire. Didn't they know... She couldn't even finish the thought. Her grandmother didn't even seem happy to see her. Maybe she was sad too. She was Daddy's Mommy.

Maybe now that it's morning she will be nicer. Maybe her grandmother will let her sit in her lap and brush her hair. Sawyer pushes her blanket off, before easing herself off the narrow bed, the wooden floor cool beneath her feet as she pads to the door. She quietly peeks out and makes her way downstairs to the kitchen.

She needed to be a good girl for her mom and dad so they could be proud of her. Maybe if she could impress her grandmother, Sawyer would feel loved again. Right now, her grandmother was all she had. No one liked a crybaby and since she was already ten-years-old, she had to keep any tears that fell to herself.

"Good morning." Her voice wobbles slightly as she fought to keep her tears at bay.

Her grandmother, already dressed, keeps her back to her. "None of that; crying won't bring them back."

Sawyer's visions of sitting on her lap dissolve like sandcastles in the tide.

She turns, unblinking, as she looks at Sawyer still in her simple nightshirt. "Go get dressed. We do not come downstairs in pajamas. You are a Sterling."

Sawyer pulls her lips into her mouth and bites down before fleeing back to the bedroom. Its bare walls are more welcoming than her only living relative is. She wishes she had never gone downstairs. She welcomes new tears.

Sawyer knows they won't bring her parents back, but she is comforted in mourning them. Her grandmother doesn't seem to feel anything at all. She pulls open the window shade to look across the now light-filled lawn and notices other houses not too far away.

Maybe there are children she can make friends with. Movement on the street below catches her eyes. A man walks down the driveway of one house to collect a newspaper from the end. He tucks it under his arm, reminding her of her daddy.

She backs away from the window and crumples back on to her bed. This bed doesn't even feel right. The sheets are starchy and too stiff, nothing like the soft flannel of her bed on the farm. Are Beau and Bess missing her? Silent sobs wrack her small frame. If she could have brought Boots, she might've felt a little better.

Holding her soft kitten, and feeling the way his purrs would rumble through his little body, always made her happy before. Would anything ever make her happy again?

"Are you dressed yet?"

The sharp shout of the words makes Sawyer jump as if struck. Her parents almost never shouted at her. The question scares her into clumsily tugging on pants and a t-shirt from her bag.

"Coming," she adds nervously.

When she walks back into the kitchen, her grandmother isn't there. Uncertain of what she should do, she hugs the edges of the room looking for an answer. When she sees a small bowl of oatmeal set out on the table, a petite glass of orange juice next to it, she somehow knows it was for her.

Oatmeal had been a regular breakfast on the farm. The only thing missing was a room full of people who loved her. Beau had probably already eaten and was playing in the orchard.

There are trees here. She saw them from the window upstairs. They were tall and slender with white bark. They didn't look like good climbing trees though. A tear rolls down her cheek, disappearing into her bowl before she can wipe it away.

She carries her now empty bowl and glass, and set them in the sink. She walks back over to the table and wonders whether she should stay in the kitchen or go back up to the newfound comfort of the room she slept in.

A throat clearing behind her interrupts her internal debate. She turns and sees her grandmother holding her purse. "I have to go somewhere, and you can't come with me. There's a peanut butter sandwich in the refrigerator for you to have at lunch. Stay inside the house. I will be back before dinner."

With that, Sawyer is alone. The large house is scary now that she is all by herself. There are old oil portraits on the walls. The eyes of Sterlings long gone seem to follow her. Coupled with the creaks and groans of an old unfamiliar house, fright ensues.

She hurries back up the stairs to the room she felt safest in. She pulls the blankets over her head and pretends this is all a dream. That somehow when she wakes up, she will be back on the farm and her parents won't be gone.

She has seen the *Wizard of Oz* with Beau and his mom in town. If she just had a pair of ruby slippers, she could be home right now. Flying monkeys and trees not fit to climb invade the happy dream she has tried to will herself into having.

Hours pass as the light from the window cast shadows across the room.

A slam of a car door alerts her to the return of her grandmother. The grumble of her stomach reminds her of the forgotten sandwich in the kitchen. She freezes. Will her grandmother be angry she has forgotten to eat it? She hurries downstairs with the hope of eating the sandwich before her grandmother gets inside.

She catches a glimpse of her walking toward the mailbox as she speeds past a window in the front room. The sandwich is cold from its time in the fridge, the peanut butter cement-like as she tries to wolf it down. She grabs her dirty glass from that morning and fills it with water from the tap in the hope it will help her swallow what is in her mouth.

She chews as fast as she can, forcing down two big bites that rub her throat painfully on the way down. She shoves the last bite into her mouth just as she hears the door open. Sawyer finally starts to relax. She has done it, there is no reason her grandmother can be upset with her.

"What are you doing in here?" her grandmother asks, flipping on a switch, immediately brightening the room.

Sawyer starts to hold up her glass. She is going to say to get some water but all her fear at upsetting her grandmother hits her again. When she opens her mouth to speak, her stomach revolts and she vomits.

Her grandmother's lip curls up as she looks at her in repulsion. "Into the bathroom now, while I clean up this mess."

Sawyer apologizes repeatedly, as she sidesteps the mess and flies up the stairs to the guest bathroom. Her shirt has seen most of the damage and she carefully drags it over her head trying not to get any in her hair. She fills the sink with hot water and retches as she tries to clean the mess from it.

The door swings open as her grandmother commands her to take off her pants and get into the tub. As she carries Sawyer's soiled clothes from the room, Sawyer hears her say something about this all being over by morning. After her bath, she is sent to bed with no dinner in case her stomach rebels again.

A firm shake of her shoulder jolts her awake the following morning. "Hurry, we need to go."

She sits up confused as she watches her grandmother's retreating figure. A glance to the window confirms it isn't even light outside. Where are they going? She changes out of her pajamas to avoid raising her grandmother's ire. Sawyer slowly makes her way down to the kitchen.

Another bowl of oatmeal and a glass of orange juice waits for her.

"I'll get your bag," her grandmother says, passing by her.

"My bag?" Sawyer asks. "Where are we going?"

Her grandmother doesn't stop to answer. Sawyer fights the desire to follow her until she answers her question, afraid of upsetting her again. She looks down at her now empty bowl, surprised she has managed to eat it all.

"Come on, Sawyer."

She leaves the bowl and glass on the table and rushes to where her grandmother is holding the front door open for her. Still confused, she hurries outside, takes the backpack her grandmother pushes in her direction, and goes to stand by the car. Maybe once they are on the road, her grandmother will tell her where they are going. A small kernel of hope expands within her. Could they be going back to the farm?

Her grandmother doesn't speak, and Sawyer sits quietly beside her. She parks near a vaguely familiar building and Sawyer realizes they are at the airport. They have to be going to the farm. Tears of joy cloud her vision as she stumbles behind her grandmother. When they get to the gate, a flight attendant comes out to talk to her.

"I have a special pin for you," she says, attaching a pin with a ribbon onto the front of her shirt.

They pinned something like this to her last time. They told her it meant she was flying by herself.

"You aren't coming to the farm with me?" Sawyer asks her grandmother.

"You aren't going back to the farm."

Her eyes open wide and her mouth drops as she realizes wherever she is going, she will be alone. "Where am I going?"

As she pats Sawyer on the head, she says gruffly, "To stay with your godmother."

The flight attendant squeezes Sawyer's hands sympathetically before standing and telling her it is time to get on the plane. Another plane? She shakes her head and cannot stop the tears from filling her eyes.

"Stop that. Now be a good girl and get on the plane," her grandmother says firmly before turning and walking away.

Sawyer lifts her hand, wanting to stop her, wanting to know what she has done wrong, wanting her grandmother not to leave her. She is gone before Sawyer can find the words to ask her to stay.

She trembles with fear at the take-off and landing, but somehow manages to sleep most of the time in between.

"Welcome to Seattle," the pilot's voice crackles over the intercom.

"Washington," she says to herself, trying to picture herself on the other side of the United States. The flight attendant walks with her out to the gate. There is a woman waiting. She is staring out the windows at the plane but turns when she sees her approach.

"Oh, Sawyer," she cries out, sinking to her knees and pulling the young girl to her chest.

Sawyer is too surprised and still overwhelmed from being on the plane to react. After she doesn't move to release her immediately, Sawyer relaxes slightly in her grasp. The woman stands slowly, clasping Sawyer's small hand in hers.

"Ready?"

"What's your name?" Sawyer asks shyly.

"She didn't tell you—" The woman shakes her head then smiles brightly. "My name is Wendy."

"Like from *Peter Pan?*" Sawyer asks.

She squeezes Sawyer's hand. "Exactly."

Sawyer follows her out to a car. "Am I going to live with you?"

"For the summer."

Sawyer stops, tensing up. "Where do I go after that?"

Wendy cringes. "I'm not sure, sweetie."

Nodding glumly, Sawyer follows her.

Sawyer is quiet as they drive. She looks around when Wendy parks. They are at a marina.

"Is this where you live?" Sawyer asks, getting out of the car.

Wendy smiles widely. "Come on. I can't wait to show you."

She carries Sawyer's bag as Sawyer follows her into the marina. There are various boats of all sizes docked here. Wendy stops suddenly in front of one of the bigger boats.

"Here she is," she gestures proudly.

A wide wooden plank acts as a ramp up on to the boat. *Don't fall*, Sawyer tells herself as she walks up it.

"Hi."

She jumps at the unexpected greeting, grabbing wildly for the railing of the boat and hurrying the rest of the way before turning to glare at its source.

A tall boy with messy brown hair watches her. "I'm Jared. What's your name?"

"Sawyer." He seems nice. She offers her hand politely.

"Ever sailed before?" he asks, shaking her hand and dropping it quickly.

She shakes her head.

"It's almost as much fun as flying."

She crinkles her nose as she thinks of her parents. "I don't like flying."

He tilts his head at her. "Good thing this boat can't fly."

Silly boy, she thinks, turning back around to look for Wendy. *Everyone knows boats can't fly.*

chapter 1

Sawyer

My best friend Sarah is getting married in a week. I'm not sure how I've managed to help plan her wedding while simultaneously trying to block it out of my mind. The distraction of organizing the small details is a welcome escape in avoiding how different things are now.

I'm happy for her. I am. *Change is good, right.* I drag myself from my comfy cocoon of blankets and pad barefoot into the kitchen.

"Dude, it's not Wednesday," Jared mumbles behind me, his voice raspy from sleep.

I pull a bowl for my cereal down from the cabinet and turn. "Huh?"

He gives me a crooked smile and points to my ass. I'm still not used to living with a guy and I hadn't thought to pull on pants after I woke up. I'm apparently wearing the wrong day of the week underwear.

"Stop looking at my ass, perv." I pull my t-shirt down as I move closer to the fridge to grab milk. I try my best to ignore the fact that Jared noticing my ass excites me.

This is Jared; the guy I spent almost every summer with after my parents died. Other people had been there too. It hadn't been some weird Blue Lagoon or Lord of the Flies thing. Even though there were always adults around, we still managed to have fun. Those summers kept me sane. That's why Jared needs to be not so attractive, especially considering he's my new roommate.

Any attraction I'm feeling has to be a symptom of the lack of sex I'm experiencing. With Sarah's wedding, Jared moving in, and life in general, I have been too busy. And it isn't helping that Jared is hotter than I remember. I move to eat my breakfast in the living room. My eyes stalk him as he gets something to eat.

His bare back to me, I admire the flex and pull of his muscles as he reaches for a glass and then the curve of his ass as he bends to grab something from the fridge. Fuck me, when did he get so hot?

He was always good-looking but in a cute way before. Cute never did anything for me. I preferred the panty-melting type of guy, and that is exactly what Jared has turned into. It would be a smart move to get some distance before I had to retire

Wednesday from my underwear drawer permanently.

I leave my half-finished bowl on the coffee table and silently flee to my room. Last thing Jared needs is me panting after him, and I'm not really panting after him. It's like having a healthy appreciation of art. Just because you appreciate a painting, it doesn't mean you need to mount it to your wall. Seriously, mounting anything is the last thing I should be picturing.

Jared is my friend, and he's had a shitty year. Sarah told me herself they had a heart-to-heart over him coming to the wedding. She had been scared that it would bring up bad memories for him. From what she said, he had been nothing but supportive, even agreeing to be part of the wedding party.

Would her wedding remind him of his own failed marriage? It was almost over before the ink dried on the marriage certificate. It had been such a rushed affair in front of the Justice of the Peace. Sarah and I weren't even there. After the baby was born, they were going to do it right and have a bigger ceremony. All those plans dissolved when Kristy lost the baby. As hard as Jared tried to do the right thing, it was a huge relief when they broke up.

Kristy wasn't bad or anything. She just wasn't good enough for Jared. As much as I had my suspicions on how accidental her pregnancy was, I wouldn't wish a miscarriage on anyone. Jared was a wreck after it happened. The only silver lining in everything that happened was being able to offer him Sarah's old room.

The few times we've gone out since he moved in, he rebuffed any girl who hit on him. I've gotten in the habit of acting like we're together when we're out. That has to be what's causing all my problems right now. Of course, I'm not meeting anyone if I look like I'm already taken. Maybe if I was getting some, I could stop eye-fucking him.

I need to get laid. I'm so going out tonight. It's been a while since I bought anything cute. I shower quickly with visions of the mall dancing in my head. I hurry to get ready.

"Where're you heading?"

I gulp and glance back at him. He's stretched out across the couch, thankfully, now fully dressed.

"I'm running to the mall."

He sits up. "Can I come with? I need a shirt for the rehearsal dinner."

My shoulders sag. There goes getting away from him. "Hurry up, sweet cheeks."

I wait while he pulls on shoes and his coat.

"Want me to drive?" he offers nonchalantly.

I smirk and shake my head. I have no idea why everyone thinks I'm such a bad driver. It's been forever since my last accident and almost a year since my last speeding ticket. Patience has never been something I had an overabundance of. If I were going somewhere, I'd rather get there sooner than later. Besides, a yellow Hummer on anyone's bumper is just incentive to get out of my way.

We knock out finding a shirt for Jared first. I make him buy the first one that looks relatively okay so I won't have to stare at how each one hugs his broad shoulders. He follows me into a trendy little shop I like. Those clothes are fun and not expensive. Part of the reason my cash has stretched as far as it has is I don't splurge that often.

Wandering around the store, I grab a few dresses to try on while Jared snags a chair just outside the dressing room.

"Are you going to model them?" he jokes, once I'm heading in.

"You want to see them?" I ask surprised.

He nods, leaning back further into his chair, getting comfortable. "You should catwalk."

I roll my eyes and shake my head as I close the dressing room door. I try on the first dress. Turns out "dress" is an over exaggeration. I'm short and this barely covers my ass. I walk out to show Jared more as joke since I can't see myself buying it. He's goofing off on his phone so I clear my throat to get his attention. I shiver, and I tell myself it's the chill from the store's AC, not the way Jared moves his eyes up my body.

When his gaze finally reaches my face, I take in his wide eyes and open mouth. Is that in reaction to me? I start to turn.

"That one." I look back at him. "Get that one," he affirms.

Seems like Jared likes what he sees. I might be seeing things, but I swear I catch him adjusting himself.

I change back into my clothes and grab the dress Jared likes and another one. I can't handle a repeat of the way he looks at me so I pray to the shopping gods that this other one fits.

He follows me to the register, standing closer than normal. The sales person snaps me out of my Jared-induced haze when she asks for my card a second time. While she rings me up, I catch her checking Jared out. I take a step back to close the distance between us. I'm being stupidly possessive of one of my best friends.

Without missing a beat, he rests his chin on the top of my head as if it's the most natural thing in the world. That's clearly all this is, a natural comfort level we have developed over years of being friends. Any desire toward him I might have felt before could potentially ruin that.

Going out tonight and picking up a honey for the evening, is just me being a good friend. Once we're back at the condo, any hopes I have for ditching him crash and burn when he invites himself out with me.

Saying no to Jared has always been nearly impossible. My whole objective for going out tonight was to get laid.

Instead, here I am ordering another shot so I hope I won't remember what a failure tonight is turning out to be. Based on Jared's reaction to the dress in the store, I assumed it would be foolproof in attracting company for the evening. I'm not expecting Jared to glare at every man who looks at me. He's easily the biggest guy in the place. So far, no one's been brave enough to approach me.

"Why are you being such a cock blocker?" I groan.

He tries to look innocent before shrugging. "These dudes are all losers. You should be thanking me."

A song I like coming on is the only thing that stops me from arguing with him. I head toward the dance floor instead, surprised when he follows me. This has to be some new level of torture. I try to imagine anyone else behind me and just lose myself in the music.

When his fingers grip my hips, I start to melt into him before remembering this is Jared. With a jolt, I step away from him. Appreciation mode only. Safer for all involved to not mount my roommate.

My goal for the night suddenly shifts from getting laid to not throwing myself at Jared Keller.

chapter 1 ½

Jared

I am being the biggest cock blocker on the planet right now. There is no way I can handle Sawyer bringing some random dude home. She might be pissed at me, but she deserves so much more than that. If there is one thing that can come from us now being roommates, it's that I can finally get her to understand how amazing she is.

The past year has given me a perspective I have not had before. I know now more than ever how my actions can have potentially life-long consequences. I went from being irresponsible with a girl I didn't love to married and expecting a baby in the blink of an eye.

Now I'm divorced and seeing the world in a completely new way. Kristy's a nice girl; and who knows, maybe if she hadn't gotten pregnant I could have grown to love her. Instead, I married her out of obligation. As scary as fatherhood seemed, I was all in, one hundred percent.

I know what it's like to grow up with separated parents. I didn't want that for my son or daughter. I was ready to be whatever Kristy needed to make sure that didn't happen to my kid. When she lost the baby, we both realized we had rushed into a marriage neither of us was ready for.

As much as I mourn the loss of the baby we will never meet, I feel shame because of the relief I felt when I knew I wasn't going to be the father to a baby whose mother I didn't love. Casual sex becomes anything but, when you accidentally knock someone up. It might annoy Sawyer, but I won't let her make the same mistakes I did.

chapter 2

Sawyer

"You snore."

Well that's a fine way to wake up. I squint across our room at Jared. He's in his bed, his head resting on his hand. Our room has two doubles. The bed and breakfast, where yesterday my best friend Sarah married Will, is on the small side. Jared and I decided to double up and share a room so there would be an extra room available for someone else.

"I do not snore." At his raised brow, I add, "I breathe loudly."

I reach over, grab my phone off the nightstand between our beds, and groan when I realize how early it is.

Jared chuckles after I cover my face with a pillow. I can hear him getting up and dressing, so I leave the pillow across my face to give him some semblance of privacy in our shared room. I hear him inhale.

"Dude, I smell bacon. Come on. Let's go get some before it's all gone."

I shift the pillow back behind my head, giving him an exaggerated pout. "I don't want to get up. Why don't you go and bring us both up a plate?"

One side of his mouth pulls up. "Not happening. Now get your lazy ass out of bed."

I've known Jared forever. After my parents died and my grandmother was saddled with me, I somehow ended up on a boat with a bunch of strangers protesting whaling. Jared's mom was both marine biologist and protestor, and brought him along for the ride.

There is nothing like pissing off the Japanese government to add some flash to a 'what I did over my summer vacation' essay. I smile to myself remembering how we drove the crew crazy that summer.

"Earth to Sawyer, bacon waits for no one," he jokes, snapping me out of my daydream.

I had slept in flannel super hero PJs. I learned the hard way a long time ago, that just because Atlanta was considered the South didn't mean it couldn't get cold as shit in the wintertime. Bummer is that it's supposed to warm up next week when we'll be back in Colorado. Jared quickly turns around when I start changing. I don't know why this bugs me. It's not as if he hasn't seen boobs before. I glance down at my chest. Sure, I'll never be called busty, but I'd gotten over that a long time ago.

I pull on some jeans that are one squat away from splitting at the knees and a fuzzy black sweater. I pop into the bathroom to make sure my hair isn't acting all crazy and brush my teeth. Jared follows me, deciding to brush his teeth as well. I hesitate before spitting paste into the sink. I feel weird spitting in front of him. I've never felt like that. As long as I've known him, I've brushed my teeth with him a million times.

I pretend as if he isn't there, which isn't easy considering how he dwarfs the small bathroom. A good foot taller than me at 6'4", Jared has always had a way of filling whatever space he occupies. He's lean though, all that snowboarding has left little room for fat on his chiseled frame.

I dated a boarder once, one of his friends, Caleb. He was shorter than Jared but all muscle. I glance at Jared again, thinking back to the last time I saw him without his shirt on.

Once we make it downstairs, I'm surprised to see how packed the dining room is considering what time the reception ended last night. Brian, Sarah's big brother, waves us over to where he and his wife, Christine, are sitting. I don't have any siblings. Brian's the type of brother that makes me wish I had one.

My stomach grumbles at his full plate. The food is set up buffet style so we go load up. I bite back a laugh at Jared's ample serving of bacon.

"So, do you think we'll see the newlyweds?" Christine asks as we sit back down.

I shake my head. "Doubtful."

Because Will is a teacher, they aren't going on their actual honeymoon until spring break. Therefore, I'm pretty sure they're going to make the most of the cabin today and tomorrow.

"You don't think they'll pop in to say goodbye to everyone?" She seems shocked.

I shrug. "I wouldn't; but when you put it that way, maybe they will."

Jared looks over at me. "You wouldn't?"

I drop my fork and shift in my chair to face him. "Hypothetically speaking, since I have zero intention of ever getting married, if it was the day after my wedding, saying goodbye to people would be the last thing on my mind."

The second after I say it, I cringe. I have filter issues sometimes, and considering Jared just got divorced, I feel like I have a mouthful of foot. If he noticed, it doesn't show. He just refocuses his attention back to his bacon.

"What time are you kids heading out?" Sarah's Uncle Chip asks, sitting down across from us.

"Our flight is at five." I tilt my head toward Brian. "Don't forget you're our ride to the airport."

The bride and groom walk in an hour later while we're lingering over coffee. They make their rounds, stopping by each table to say hello until they reach ours. I have to smile when Will pulls out her chair. They're good together. I'm happy for Sarah even though part of me is mourning her loss. I've been replaced. I'm still getting used to having Jared as a roommate. He took over her half of the condo after she decided to move to Atlanta to be with Will.

I'm hoping now that the wedding is over and once I'm back in Denver, I can get rid of the unsettled feeling that's been gnawing at me. I've never been one for routine, but I'm suddenly craving it. Jared relinquishes his seat to Sarah so she can sit next to me. Whereas Jared might be my oldest friend, Sarah is my best. I'll never forget meeting her on that train to Jersey. We've been somewhat inseparable ever since.

In an effort to be stealthy, she leans over and whispers in my ear, "What's going on with you and Jared?"

Huh? "Um, nothing."

She smirks. "I call bullshit on that. You guys seem different."

I have to pause to consider what she just said. Have I been acting differently? I'm excited we're living together. I feel bad that his marriage ended, but his ex wasn't my favorite person, so I'm not sad to see her out of his life. Maybe I have been consciously trying to look nice around him. I haven't bummed around the condo rocking a mud mask since he moved in. I'm not really sure why. Nothing would have stopped me from doing it before.

I look back at her. "You don't think I have a thing for him, do you?"

I follow her eyes as they find him, across the room, probably getting another serving of bacon. It's Jared. He's a great guy. I've known him forever. Sure, he's hot, like panty dropping hot, but there has to be a reason nothing ever happened between us. I'm an old pro at the whole friends with benefits concept, and I never got that vibe from him. Maybe Sarah's just in an oversexed-induced haze and she is seeing things that aren't there. I wish I were in an oversexed situation. I'm currently in a record-breaking dry spell.

"For someone so observant, you are fucking blind," she murmurs before swiping a mini muffin off my plate.

"I was going to eat that," I grumble, outwardly ignoring her comment.

My eyes are drawn to Jared as he makes his way back to our table. Sarah kisses my cheek and gets up so he can have his chair back while she goes and gets a plate of her own. I've never been one to think too much before I leap, and I don't like the way her comments are making me feel.

Throwing caution to the wind, I lean over and rest my hands on his shoulder to pull him down closer to me. My lips are a breath away from his earlobe. "I think we should fuck."

With a loud gulp, he swallows whatever he had been chewing and looks at me. I haven't moved. My hands are still on his shoulder, so we're almost nose-to-nose.

"You've said some crazy shit over the years, but that's gotta be my favorite." He flashes me a crooked grin.

"I'm being serious." I'm offended. Usually, when I come on to a guy, it's better received.

He just shakes his head, turning it back to his plate. I drop my hands from his shoulder and have to accept the fact that maybe he isn't interested in me that way. I now blame Sarah for even putting the idea in my head. I'm contemplating my revenge when Jared bumps my shoulder with his and asks me if I'm done eating. I nod and follow him back up to our room. I've wrapped our awkward silence around myself like a blanket, wishing for once in my life I had kept my mouth shut.

I'm barely in the door when he's on me. The flipped switch is such a shock to my system that I push him away to ask him what the hell he's doing.

My back is to the door. He has a hand resting on either side of my face. I'm trying to catch my breath as I look up into wild hazel eyes.

He drops one hand, sliding it down my arm until my hand is in his and pulls it to the front of his jeans. "I have been rock fucking hard since you said what you said. Please let me know if you were just fucking around."

"I wasn't fucking around," I whisper as I press my hand further against his impressive bulge.

His lips find mine, and I grin against them. I'm so getting laid. I fumble with his belt and push his jeans down. When I realize he isn't wearing boxers, I get even more turned on just thinking about him going commando. I stroke him, loving the way his hips jerk when I tighten my grasp around him or rub my thumb across its head. He steps out of his socks, shoes, and jeans, now naked from the waist down. He picks me up, walks me over to his bed, and drops me on it. I look up at him as he slips off my ankle boots and socks before unfastening and easing my jeans down my legs.

Scrambling to my knees, I pull off my sweater and crawl over to help him take off his shirt. This isn't the first time I've seen him without a shirt, it's just the first time I've gotten to touch his bare skin. I've always loved his chest piece. Shoulder to shoulder, his first love, the Rockies. He returns the favor and cups my breasts in his hands, rolling his thumbs over my nipples. I'm not top heavy and don't always wear a bra. As good as all of this feels, I'm ready for the main act.

I reach down with both hands and pull him cock first onto the bed with me.

"Let me grab a condom," he groans.

"I'm clean, and I have a birth control thinger in my arm," I pant, not letting him go.

A mixture of emotions crosses his face before he rubs his hands over it. "I trust you, I do. I just have to wear one."

I feel like an asshole. His ex, the miscarriage. Of course, he'd want to be extra safe. For a beat, I'm nervous I've ruined the mood. My hands drop, and I watch him go over to the door to fish his wallet out from his jeans. He pulls a condom from it, and has it open and on, before he's back to me, covering me.

He hesitates, and I ask, "What are you waiting for?"

"You're so small. I don't want to hurt you."

I grab his face so I can look him in the eye. "I'm not gonna break and I kinda like it rough, so how about you go ahead and pound the shit out of me?"

Turns out Jared can follow directions nicely. He lets out a guttural groan as he impales me. Being flexible turns out to be helpful as that boy thoroughly fucks me. What's so freeing is how much trust I have in him. When he lifts me, turns me, or positions me,

I can just relax and go with it. I can only hope the wedding guests in the rooms around us are still downstairs eating. I've never been quiet, but holy shit, Jared has me speaking different languages.

The noises he makes are just as hot. With one hand pulling my hair, another massaging my clit, he rams me from behind. His mouth is at my ear, telling me how fucking hot I am. That boy is the orgasm whisperer.

"Shit, if I knew you could fuck like that, I would've said something sooner," I joke afterward, sprawled out on top of him as I try to catch my breath.

I get up to take a shower. Once I'm out, he goes in to take his. I curl up on my bed and doze until he comes out all wet and manly looking. If we had more time, I'd be game for another round. He's quiet while he gets dressed. I do not attempt to hide the fact that I'm watching him.

It's weird that he's so quiet, though. Normally, he'd be making fun of me or something. "Everything cool?"

He scratches the back of his head. "I'm processing what we just did."

"I know. We can't even blame it on having too much to drink," I hedge, hoping he doesn't regret it.

"So what do we blame it on?" He sounds annoyed.

32

"Our combined overall yumminess," I give him a saucy wink and am relieved when he smiles.

Sex has never been a big deal to me. I know plenty of people hung up on the notion that you have to be in love to make love. More power to them. I like to fuck. They would probably call me a slut. I don't really care. There isn't a lot of drama in my life. I don't believe in cheating, so if a guy I think is hot has a girlfriend, I don't hit on him. If I'm getting busy with someone on a regular basis and find myself interested in someone else, I tell him. I think as long as you stay honest in your relationships with people that you're going to be fine.

My only concern at this point is my relationship with him being different. I don't want that. I just want him to keep being my friend with a little something-something on the side. I hate how awkward the silence feels as we pack. I go to grab my bag, but he stops me, carrying it for me. He's never done that before.

"Don't act different, Jar," I fume, tugging my bag from his grasp. "Just because we had sex doesn't mean I can't carry my own shit."

"No matter what you say or want, it's gonna be different," he says, his hand on the doorknob.

"But why?" I argue.

"'Cause all I can think about now is being inside you." He pulls open the door and walks out into the hall.

I watch, mouth open, as the door slowly closes between us. Shit. Now all I can think about is him inside me. I squeeze my thighs together and shake my head. Keep it in your pants, Sawyer. When I manage to open the door and make it into the hallway, I kick myself for not letting him carry my bag. It's kind of heavy. When I make it to the main entrance, I see his suitcase by the door and set mine next to it. I'm about to go off in search of him when I run into Will's mom.

"You weren't going to leave without saying goodbye?" she asks, pulling me into a hug.

"No, Mama Price. I would never do that." I tilt my head so it rests on her shoulder.

"I told Sarah you need to move closer. You could always live with me," she adds hopefully.

"I promise to visit a lot. Trust me. You'll be sick of me." I watch Jared approach us with Brian by his side. "I'm just not done with Denver yet."

She playfully tugs my hair. "Back to pink?"

I shrug. It was red a few months back, and the pink is now more an under color than all over. "What color should I do next?"

She shakes her head. "I like the blonde with the pink. You should keep it like this."

I kiss her cheek. "Sounds like a plan. How was Italy?"

She gets a faraway look in her eyes. "Belissimo."

I narrow mine at her. "Did you get laid?"

Will's mom has come a long way from the woman I met this past summer. She was a shell; coiled in on herself and holding on to grief so tightly she pushed everyone else away. She swats my arm and laughs before kissing my forehead and saying she'll never tell. I so have to talk to Will. His mama got lucky on vacation.

Before, she barely spoke and she wouldn't even leave her house when I came to stay with her. She seems so different now, happy. I know she regrets her part in Will and Sarah's time apart. Grief can make you do crazy things. It's almost understandable for a woman whose daughter and husband were both taken before their time. That's another reason why I'll never get married or have kids. Not for me.

She waves goodbye and walks away when Brian and Jared reach me. I stare after her, grinning. Jared catches my eye, and I wonder if he thinks I'm smiling about what happened earlier. My face gets hot when I think about what he said.

He makes a face at me when I don't stop Brian from carrying my bag to his car. I ignore him. The only reason I cared is that he hadn't carried my bag when we got here. I didn't want him to change just because we had sex.

"Hey!"

I turn and see Sarah jogging in my direction. I open my arms to receive her impending hug. She is happier than I've ever seen her. I relax in our hug, trying not to think about how much I'll miss her face. Yeah, we'll text and call, but it's already different.

I find her ear. She'll love this. "Jared and I did it after breakfast."

She pulls back, her hands on my shoulders, mouth open. Her eyes flick to Jared's back and then to mine again. "You're joking."

I smirk. I don't joke. Well, I do, just not about sex.

Her eyes widen. "Oh, my God, you did."

I glance over at Jared and shush her when I see he's turned to look at us. He raises an eyebrow. Shit, he totally knows I just told her.

Her voice pulls my eyes away from him. "You need to call me the second you get home and tell me everything."

I nod, leaning in to give her another squeeze. "I love you."

"I love you too, babe."

I let Jared ride up front because he has longer legs. I roll down my window to blow Sarah a kiss as we pull away.

"Everything," she calls out one last time.

chapter 2 ½

Jared

When I first met Sawyer, I was bummed she wasn't a boy. Who wanted to spend the summer on a boat with a girl? I'm all for it now, especially after how we spent the morning. Girls were still weird back then. A boy would have been so much cooler. I had visions of playing pirates.

All the girls I knew played with dolls. I had another thing coming. The first week at sea wasn't much fun. Sawyer cried a lot and my mom spent way more time with her than me. I was not impressed. Sure, I knew her parents died, but I had never experienced anything like that.

The second week we were on the boat, she cried less and kept following me around. It was annoying, being stuck with a girl. That all changed when I caught her playing a prank on the cook. She was so small she could sneak stuff out of the kitchen right under his nose.

I figured hers was a useful skill to have, so I recruited her. It wasn't long before she was bossing me around. I got used to it. She always had a knack for getting me to do what she wanted. Guess some things never change in that aspect. By the end of that summer, I wouldn't trade her for ten boys. She was the coolest girl I had ever known.

Maybe it was because she grew up on a farm. She was different from the girls back home. Nothing scared her. I almost pissed myself when a whale surfaced not far from the boat when we were on the main deck, but not Sawyer. For a minute, as she leaned over the rail, she seemed ready to jump in and swim with him.

Sometimes it bugged me that everyone liked her more than me. Something about her made everyone around her want to take care of her. I might have hated her if I hadn't wanted to make her smile instead. That should have been my first clue.

How long have I fantasized about Sawyer Sterling? I let go of any illusions of anything ever happening between us a long time ago. I was so sure that I was permanently friend-zoned. I glance back at her. Brian's talking about some snowboarding Xbox game, maybe skateboarding. Lawyers play Xbox? Sawyer's eyes move from the window to mine. Shit, I look away even though she just caught me staring at her.

I just had sex with Sawyer fucking Sterling. Hot fucking sex. All I can think about is burying myself in her again. At first, I was sure she was joking, just pulling some stupid shit to fuck with my head. She doesn't lie, though. Even if it sucks, she says what she thinks.

She's the coolest girl I've ever known. I sure as shit hope we didn't just fuck up our friendship. I've learned the hard way how bad it sucks when you can't trust someone. What if it was just a one-time thing to her? Fuck. Living with her will seriously suck ass if that's true.

God; and all that yoga she does in the living room. It's already hard enough to watch her do that and now that I know what her legs feel like wrapped around my waist... I don't think I can ever idly watch her do that again.

Attempting to look casual, I glance back at her. Is she being quiet because Brian is in the car? I want to know what she's thinking. How do I ask without sounding like a pussy? No, she started this, and I don't want to do anything to push her away. I'll let her make the first, er, second move. I can wait.

chapter 3

Sawyer

Awkward silence. Awesome. I glance over at Jared. Nothing better than a silent travel companion. Watching the flight attendant hit on him is fun too. You don't care, I repeat to myself. You don't care. Problem is, I kind of do.

"Want me to drive?"

I blink at him, realizing we're standing at my Hummer. Guess I spaced out. "No, I'll drive. Buckle up."

I love my car, truck, whatever my little monster is. It makes me feel big, so I totally believe that over compensating theory. I climb in and start thinking about Jared's truck and his package. That theory definitely doesn't apply to him. He's one hundred percent proportionate. The delicious ache between my thighs is reminder enough. I autopilot it home. If I speed or change lanes too often Jared doesn't mention it. I have patience problems.

Once we're inside, we retreat to our separate corners. The washer and dryer are closer to my room. We meet there, travel laundry in tow.

"You can go first," he says, turning around.

"Stop right there," I demand, dropping my basket. "This," I gesture between the two of us, "needs to stop feeling weird. Don't act differently. Got it?" I take a step closer to him, and he lets his mesh laundry bag fall to the ground. "You don't have to carry my bags. You don't have to let me go first."

His hands lift to cradle my face. "What if I just want to take care of you?"

I snake my arm around his neck and stand on my tiptoes as I lower his mouth to mine. "I take care of myself."

I'm lifted, turned, and pressed against the wall. His lips are confusingly soft and demanding at the same time. I push back, threading my fingers into his hair and tug hard until he groans. This, right here; this is my drug. I sense it in every single one of my pores. He wants me. I grind my hips against him.

My lips move to his ear. "I'm so wet."

He doesn't need any more encouragement. His lips attack mine as he carries me to my room. He pauses only long enough to pull my bag off my bed before dumping me on it.

"Have any condoms in here?"

I nod to my bedside table before shimmying out of my clothes. He chuckles at my assortment of naughtiness as he grabs one. I crawl over to him, pluck it out of his hands, and hold it in my mouth while I unfasten his jeans and free him. He tugs his shirt off over his head as I slide his jeans down his legs. His eyes are hooded as he watches me handle him. I've always loved cocks. There is something so foreign about them. They make me curious.

I like that a simple touch of my fingertip can make his hips jerk. He's all man, but here I feel powerful. I palm his balls with one hand and reach up to tear open the foil packet held between my teeth. Somehow, he gets harder. The groan that escapes his lips as I roll the condom onto him excites me. I'm hoping for a repeat of this morning. With any luck, I'll be walking funny tomorrow.

His hesitation from earlier is gone. He has no issues manhandling me. Before long, I'm facedown, ass up, getting pounded. My pillow does nothing to muffle my pleas of, "Harder, harder."

Once we're thoroughly fucked and the second condom is disposed of, Jared pulls me against his chest, his hands slowing trailing up and down my back. I pull away. I'm not a cuddler. Jared's eyes follow me as I pull on a robe and walk out of my room, leaving him there, naked, in my bed.

I'm starting my laundry when he finally comes to find me. He's pulled his jeans back on but not his shirt.

"What was that?" he asks, his brows furrowed.

My right shoulder pops up as I look over at him. "What?"

He shakes his head. "You just got up and left."

I close the lid and turn, facing him all the way. "I figured we were finished."

"Not even close." He lifts me, setting me on the washer, and opens my robe.

Mission accomplished, I think, gingerly getting out of bed. I absolutely will be walking funny today. I head straight for the bathroom and fill the tub. I have aches in places I wasn't sure had muscles. I crack the window to let some steam escape, enjoying the chill. As cold as I was in Atlanta, I welcome the chill in Colorado. There is snow on the ground. It's supposed to be cold. I leave it open while I brush my teeth, closing it before I ease myself into the tub.

I'm about to doze off when there's a knock on the bathroom door. "Who is it?"

Jared pops his head in.

"I could have been on the toilet," I mumble, making no effort to cover myself.

"I heard the water." He grins, his hands already working on the button of his jeans.

"No way." I put my hand up, stopping him. "I need a recovery day before the next rodeo, cowboy."

I laugh at his pout.

"All right, no sex. Can I still get in?"

I must look confused because he asks, "What?"

I rest my arms on the edge of the tub and lay my cheek on them. "Why do you want to get in if we aren't going to have sex?"

He taps his mouth with his index finger, like he's thinking about it. "Bubble bath with a hot naked chick is kind of a no brainer. Besides, maybe I can play with your boobs and talk you into a hand job."

That makes me smile. I shift forward and motion for him to climb in. He undresses quickly and slides in behind me.

I settle against him and pass him my body soap. "If you're playing with my tits, you might as well wash them."

The rest of the week goes like that. We get comfortable, but not too comfortable. One night, I have to remind Jared he has his own bed. For a minute, I wonder if that bothers him, but he just gets dressed and pinches my nipple before going back to his room. Most days, I don't see him until after dinner. He teaches lessons at a local ski resort in the morning and then boards the rest of the day. I'm sitting on the sofa watching TV with my laptop in my lap when he walks in.

"I ordered Chinese," I say, looking up.

"Sweet." He shrugs off his coat and hangs it on the back of a stool.

He makes himself a plate and walks over to sit by me. "What're you doing?" he asks between bites.

I open my mouth for one and hold his gaze as he feeds me some sweet and sour chicken. Once I'm done chewing, I answer, "Checking flights. I have some friends staying in Fiji. They have a spare room if I want to come chill for a couple weeks."

I open my mouth for another bite and pout when he ignores me. "What friends?"

I get up and head to the kitchen for a refill. "Remember Jase?"

"Didn't you date him?"

I don't look back at him while I reload my plate. "It wasn't anything serious."

"Have you ever been serious with anyone?" Jared mumbles. The way he says it is more a statement than a question.

"Are you annoyed at me for something?" I ask, turning to walk back to the sofa.

He sets his plate down and takes mine from me, setting it on the coffee table. "I think we should date."

"Shut up," I laugh. When his face stays serious, my mouth drops. "You can't be serious. You just got divorced. The last thing you need to do is jump into something. Besides, I'm not what you want."

He picks his plate back up and turns to watch TV. "You don't know what I want."

I push at his shoulder. "Over dramatic much? I'm looking out for you, like a friend. You deserve so much more than I have to offer."

His plate is down again and his mouth is on mine before I have a chance to react. Whatever disagreement we had is forgotten the second his hands are on me. He pulls me into his lap, his teeth on my nipple through my shirt. His hands are on me, one on my ass and the other in my hair. I fumble at his jeans, stroking him once I have them open. He stands, turning us around so my back is to the cushions and undresses me from the waist down.

Jared kneels in front of me. He puts his hands under my ass and lifts my body to his mouth. Holy fuck. I've never been that into foreplay. Always been a main act kind of girl, but when he goes down on me, I forget who I am. He's above me, looking down at me. His eyes are locked on mine. All I can do is clutch at the cushions behind me, and let go. After I do let go, he slowly lowers me. I'm half on, half off the sofa. He slides a condom on while I catch my breath before pulling me the rest of the way down onto him.

His hands lift and lower me. My arms are around his neck as we kiss. I can taste myself. He slams me down harder onto his cock. Whatever pace he had tried to set before is lost. I feel it. I feel him lose control. Our lips part and I press my forehead to his as he slams me over and over again. I know what he had been trying to do. He'd tried to be soft and sweet in the beginning, but I just don't do that.

When his motions become more frantic, his breathing becomes labored; I know he's close. I lick his lip, suck it into my mouth, and bite it. He pushes into me hard one last time and groans against my mouth, his lip still trapped between my teeth. I smile, releasing it, and laugh. I'm still wearing my shirt, and he's still fully dressed.

"What's so funny?" he asks, nuzzling into my neck.

I trace my hand up his thigh and feel him twitch inside me. "You never even took off your jeans."

He presses wet kisses up my neck to my ear. His hands move to the hem of my shirt. His lips only stop touching my neck as he pulls my shirt off me. I arch my back as the rough pads of his thumbs stroke my nipples. He reaches back to push the coffee table away from the sofa and lies down, pulling me with him.

"If this is turning into round two, you're wearing too much." I laugh and tug at his shirt.

He leaves me for a minute to undress and toss the used condom. When he returns, he's naked and gloriously hard. I know this is just sex, but his body may be ruining me for anyone else.

"Do you ever sleep with more than one person at a time?"

I tilt my head. "Like a threesome?"

Jared shakes his head. "Like what we're doing."

"Oh." I think about it. "Not really. Once it stops being fun, I move on."

He lowers himself onto me. "Things aren't supposed to be fun all the time."

"Why not?" I ask, trailing my hands up his arms to his shoulders.

His weight feels delicious on me, a pleasant pressure that covers me. His skin is warm against mine. I don't want to talk. I want to feel. I capture his lips with mine, ending any more discussion. Afterward, I pluck my plate from the coffee table and rest it on his chest to finish my dinner. If he's annoyed, he doesn't show it.

"Are you still thinking about going to see that Jase guy?" Jared asks, rinsing his plate.

He passes it to me, and I load it into the dishwasher. "Maybe. Now that Sarah's wedding is all done, I feel like I'm just bumming around. I need to do something."

"What happened to that yoga place?" He passes me a glass.

"It won't open for another couple months. The contractor can email me if anything comes up."

It's my little project, my own studio. The space is simple. It's the end unit of a strip mall fifteen minutes from the condo. I'm having the space sectioned off into three areas, a large room for yoga classes and two smaller rooms, one for a masseuse, another for facials. I plan on teaching the basic yoga class a few times a week and already have some friends lined up to cover the rest. There isn't really anything I can do there right now, so why not get out of Dodge?

I pause, glass in hand, and lean against the counter. "Do you want to go?"

He cuts off the water. "It's kind of my peak season."

I place the glass in the top rack and close the dishwasher. "Of course. Silly of me to ask."

I start to walk away, but he stops me. "Let me check at work tomorrow."

"No big deal," I add.

He turns me so I'm facing him and lifts my chin. "I'd like to go with you. Let me see what I can do."

I nod, regretting even mentioning it. If we aren't careful, we might trick ourselves into thinking what we have is something when it isn't. I don't want him to become attached to an idea that will never happen. I'm comfortable, I'm familiar, I'm awesome, and he's still getting over all that bullshit with his ex. I have no illusions that he's actually interested in me. That's not how this works. This is sex.

chapter 3 ½

Jared

I didn't really need to check with anyone at work; I make the schedule. It would just be a dick move to leave them hanging when it's busy. As long as there are people willing to cover without bitching about it, I'll go. Am I being jealous? Yes. I don't care if this Jase dude is already with someone else.

We haven't discussed what we're doing. I sure as fuck don't want to push her. I've known her long enough to know what will happen if I do. She'll bail. I don't know where she'll go, but she'll take off. I'm on to her, though, as long as I don't do anything stupid.

I swap my beginner lesson with Carl for his intermediate group. I need a couple trips down the mountain to clear my head. It's early, and it snowed a bit last night. I like it this way, before it's all packed down and cut up from other people's boards and skis.

Besides, this early on a weekday, it's not as busy. I don't have to watch out for other people. The slope is mine. I'm looking for speed. I want my heart racing and my brain only focused on not wiping out. I ease up as I near the bottom. There are some posers grouped up at the bottom of the hill. Idiots. That's a stupid place to stand and chat.

I swoop past them. "Move," I growl, laughing when they jump.

Teenagers, they have an almost empty mountain to shred and they're just standing around doing nothing. I shake my head; just like I did nothing for years, even though I wanted Sawyer for myself.

chapter 4

Sawyer

"Do you even still want me to come?"

I giggle at Jared's question considering our current location. He has me bent over the vanity in my bathroom. I know he's talking about Fiji, but he did just say come while he was inside me. He groans and pulls my hips back hard.

Afterward, I answer, "I wouldn't have asked if I hadn't meant it."

He hesitates, like he doesn't believe me.

"Look, Jared. I don't get why this seems confusing for you. If you want to come, come. If you don't, well...don't."

His eyes meet mine in the mirror. "I think I should stay here." He trails his fingertip down my spine, making my knees shake, and walks out of the room.

My mouth drops as I watch him leave. What just happened? Does he want me to beg him to go? That isn't ever going to happen, ever. It's as if he doesn't even know me. I throw on some yoga pants and a t-shirt and think about calling Sarah. I decide not to. This is stupid. This right here is exactly why I don't date. All it does is complicate shit. He doesn't want to go that's his fucking problem. Who the fuck doesn't want to go to Fiji?

I open my laptop to email Jase when I notice a new unread one from my grandmother's attorney. I open it without a second thought to learn my only living relative on the planet, my grandmother, has died. I push my computer away from me and have to consider if I actually feel anything about it. Do I have any emotion knowing she has died?

Not finding any, I pull the computer back and finish reading the email. He is the executer of her estate, but as her sole heir, he needs me to go to New Hampshire and clean out her house. There goes Fiji. I open an internet browser and buy a ticket.

"I didn't mean it."

I look up to see Jared standing in my doorway. "You didn't mean what?"

"I want to go with you, if you still want me to."

I snap my laptop shut and pull my knees up to my chest. "Trip's off. My grandmother died. I have to go to New Hampshire to clean out her house."

He crosses the room and pulls me into his arms, his mouth in my hair. "I'm so sorry, Sawyer."

I pull away and slide off my bed. He trails after me as I hurry into the kitchen. "I barely knew her."

I pull a beer out of the fridge. I hand it to him to open. Then I take a healthy gulp after he hands it back to me.

"I don't remember you mentioning her." He pulls another beer out for himself.

"She's the reason we met," I say after another drink. "She didn't want a kid so she conned your mom into watching me."

"You know my mom loves you," Jared says, rubbing my arm.

I raise my beer. "Come on. Don't you know? Everyone loves me," I pause, "except for her."

He pulls me against him, and this time I don't fight it. Why do I even care?

"I'll go with you."

I pull back and look at him. "You don't have to."

He tucks my head back under his chin. "Shut up, Sawyer."

Three days later, we pull up to my grandmother's house in Hanover, New Hampshire. It's a sprawling three-story Victorian with a widow's walk.

"Here we are," I say, stating the obvious.

I let Jared carry our bags while I search for the hidden key the lawyer promised would be hidden under a potted plant. He failed to mention there were fifteen potted plants on the front porch. Jared holds the screen door open for me while I introduce the key to the lock. It appears as though they have not previously met.

The house is exactly as I remember it, shocking given the two days total I had spent there almost fourteen years ago. As if the déjà vu wasn't already powerful enough, the smell really did it. It still smelt like Old English furniture polish and stale potpourri.

I grab my bag and head upstairs. Jared is right behind me. I take the front guest room and have him put his luggage in the room across from the hall bath. He pauses by my door before moving forward to his room.

I drop my bag and follow him. "Want to order a pizza for dinner or run to the grocery store tonight?"

He falls back onto the double bed. The springs groan loudly. "Pizza sounds good."

I hit his foot. "Are you going to nap? Come on. Let's check out the place."

He makes a production of getting up before following me downstairs. My grandmother, my father's mother, hadn't been a hoarder, but she also hadn't followed the whole minimalist approach to design. Each room was full of antique, New England style wooden furniture. The stuff you see on Antiques Roadshow, not my style at all. I've held on to a few silly keepsakes over the years. Otherwise, I'm all clean lines and uncluttered spaces.

I walk around from room to room on the main floor. I have no clue what I'm going to do with all of this stuff. I don't even know if she has anything of my dad's.

Jared follows me. "What's the game plan?"

I lean in closer to check the signature on a painting in the living room. "The lawyer gave me the number of an appraiser and an auction house that can handle the pricing and selling of everything. I'm just supposed to go through the house first to see if there is anything I want."

"Do you want any of the furniture?" he asks, running his hand across the back of a dining room chair.

"I don't know. It all feels too grown up for me. I wonder if I should ask Sarah if she wants any of it." I mimic his movement and run my hand across the back of the chair opposite of him. "It seems well made."

"Want me to text her while you look through stuff?" He reaches for his phone.

"Sure. I'm going to look around some more. Can you order the pizza too?"

I walk away before he answers.

Room by room, I wander through her house.

She never wanted me. Why should I want any of her stuff?

The main floor is made up of six rooms: a parlor, a formal dining room, the kitchen, a library, a breakfast room, and a den that had been converted into a first floor master at some point over the years. The breakfast room is easy. There isn't much in it. I figure it can be the place in the house where I put anything I might want.

Going through everything in the library is daunting, with floor-to-ceiling bookshelves on three of the four walls. The fourth wall is devoted to a large picture window that overlooks the front drive. There aren't just books on the shelves but little knick-knacks here and there as well. Some of the books look old, like first edition old.

"Whoa," I hear.

I turn to watch Jared walk in. "I know, right? There's no way I can go through everything."

He walks between the overstuffed armchairs to come stand by me; he gives my hand a squeeze. "You got me. We'll just go shelf by shelf until the pizza gets here."

As much as I love books, while knowledge is power and all that, I don't have the space for a library of them. Besides, with the exception of some keepsakes, including an oversized monkey I seriously need to donate to Goodwill, I don't have many possessions. I like the idea of taking off with all of my earthly possessions in a bag. I'm not crazy about being too tied down to anything. My condo is a big deal, owning something. It seemed less of a big deal when Sarah split the cost with me, like it was just an overpriced apartment.

Now that I've gotten used to that, I'm branching out with the yoga studio. That feels like a commitment because people are depending on me. With the condo, if I had to bail, Sarah would have been cool about it. The place is paid off now, so even if I left, Jared wouldn't need me to live there. The studio is different. It's in a strip mall. I can't buy the space. I just lease it. I'm tied to a monthly commitment and employees. I could probably hire someone to do that. I just haven't been able to.

I'm lost in my thoughts when Jared clears his throat. "I'm sorry. I didn't hear you."

He holds a book up, his eyes cautious. "Dude, I think I found your dad's high school yearbook."

I rush over to him, eyes wide. I sink right to the rug-covered floor with the book in my hand, and Jared sits with me. The book is bound in navy blue leather and wide gold letters across the front spine: Hanover High School, 1979.

"I think he graduated in '79," I say, flipping to the senior class and looking for his name, Henry Sterling.

My fingers ghost over his face when I find him staring back at me with teenage eyes. He was handsome and popular, guessing from the number of signatures crowding each page. He was on his way to Dartmouth, where he would meet my mom his junior year. Dartmouth was practically in his backyard. For my mom, it was an ocean away.

She was Dutch, studying abroad. I seemed to get all my physical traits from her. I am naturally blonde, with pale blue eyes, and petite like her. My father was tall and broad with dark brown hair and eyes.

Sometimes I wonder if I had looked more like him, would my grandmother have kept me. It didn't matter anymore, though. You can't go back. You can't become too attached. When the doorbell rings, Jared leaves to pay for the pizza. I go to the shelf he had been looking at to see if there are any other yearbooks. When I see that there aren't any others, I take this one into the breakfast room and set it on the table. I want this.

"Do you want to eat in here or in the library?" Jared asks, putting a slice for me onto a plate.

"Here's good. Thanks for taking care of the pizza." I stand on my toes and kiss his cheek when I grab my plate.

"You can pay me back later," he replies in a way that tells me he isn't talking about money.

Once we're done eating, we work in the library until I'm too tired to stand. Jared carries me upstairs.

His lips on my neck revive me. Apparently, I have a debt to pay.

The next morning, I wake blanketed by Jared. I'm surprised I slept so well. I usually like my space when I sleep. For some reason, last night doesn't bug me. I take the opportunity to watch him as he sleeps; his face is so close to mine. I reach up and trace the scar that runs just to the side of his left eye. When he was fifteen, he had been jumped by some older kids at his school and was hit in the face with a board. He was in the hospital for three days. His dad pulled him out and homeschooled him after that happened.

I wonder about him, how he's so good at taking hurdles in stride. This time last year, he was married with a baby on the way. How does that not affect him? My pondering is interrupted when his weight shifts in a way for me to make my escape. The bathroom is my first stop before I head downstairs to make some tea. I poke around the kitchen thinking about what we'll need from the grocery store. I'm halfheartedly making a list when Jared walks in.

"Tea?" I ask, standing.

He nods before lifting his arm and yawning into his elbow. "Dude, I'm beat. We didn't even stay up that late."

I arch a brow over my shoulder. "I wore you out?" I ask, joking.

He comes up behind me, wrapping his arms around my waist as I turn the stove on to heat the kettle. "You must have."

After the tea, he takes a shower, and I call Sarah back. She had offered to come up and help, but I know Will would probably come too and then it would feel couple-y, and I don't want that. I don't want Sarah giving me a look every time Jared does something sweet around me. That is something coupled up people don't get about wanting to be single. They don't understand that some people actually want to be single.

Even if I ever end up in something long term with someone, I don't want to get married. What's the point? A piece of paper that holds some sort of magic claim that it will last forever or until death. I'd believe it more if the divorce rate weren't so high.

Either way, she knows Jared and I are having sex. I don't need her getting any ideas that it's more than what it is. I catch her up on what we're doing here and ask her if they need any furniture. She seems interested in the dining room set and mentions Jared had texted last night but forgot to send a picture.

She asks again if I need her to come up. When I tell her it's cool because Jared is here, she gets very quiet. This, right now, is what I was trying to avoid in person. She thinks something is up. I tell her again that it's not. When I hear the water from Jared's shower shut off, I end the call. I take and text her a pic of the dining room set on my way upstairs.

He's standing in the bathroom with a towel wrapped around his waist while he shaves.

"I like you scruffy," I say, coming up behind him and laying my cheek on his warm back.

"I'd look stupid if I stopped now," he replies as he keeps going.

I stay there in a standing-lean on him. I feel the muscles of his back lift and fall as he moves his arms. That and the lingering steam of his shower relax me. I feel like going back to bed, but there is still so much for us to do. When I don't feel the muscles move in his back for a minute, I lift my head. He turns, pulling me flush to him.

"I should shower," I say, not moving.

"Want me to get you all dirty first?" he asks, his hands gripping my ass.

My hands move to his towel and I unwrap him, letting it fall to the floor. I'm not opposed to bathroom sex but don't stop him when he picks me up and carries me back to my room.

A small part of me thrills in having sex in my grandmother's house. She was so uptight. Even from a distance, I could feel her disapproval most of my life. I think I have lived out loud because of her. Some people wonder, "What would Jesus do?" Instead, I wonder, what wouldn't Agnes Sterling do?

Much later, we head to the local Stop and Shop. This isn't the first time Jared and I have bought groceries together. He claims cart-driving duty the second we're inside the store. He's always said it's because I can't see over the cart. I'm short but not that short. Still, I've come to let him win this battle. We get some stares as we make our way around the store. I do tend to stick out. I'm used to it and meet any stares head on, a saucy grin plastered on my face.

I weigh maybe a buck ten, and even though I have Sasquatch with me, I like to think it's my "take no prisoners" stare that makes oglers back down. As we wait in line, Jared tugs me against him, tucking me between the cart and him. I lean against him, ignoring how couple-y it seems. I tell myself I'm tired from walking all over the store; not that I like hearing the thump of his heart, and that the way he smells relaxes me. Nope, it's not that.

There is a moment when Jared starts to pay, but I stop him. My hand is on his arm, reminding him that he bought the pizza last night. His hesitation bugs me for some reason. When we're unloading the rental car, I carry a stupid amount of bags. The plastic cuts into my forearms and through my winter coat in some insane need to show Jared I can take care of myself. I hate that he still carries more. Once the groceries are put away, we take packets of mini muffins into the library and pick up where we ended last night.

I keep anything that seems to have something to do with my dad. There are a couple of framed photos and a small clay pot with his initials cut into the bottom. Those join the yearbook in the breakfast room. I hesitate over a Bible, a family Bible with dates of births, weddings, and deaths carefully scribed in the back by more than one hand. Religion scares me, being somewhat of an outsider and being friends with many so-called misfits. I've seen how unaccepting those who claim faith in a higher power can be.

I keep it, anyway, as a record of my father's life. We break for lunch after finishing that room. Jared makes us sandwiches that we eat with chips while we figure out which room to do next. I'm thinking the dining room will be the easiest. After she saw the pics, Sarah called dibs on the set and had arranged for a shipping company to come pick them up. I want to have the china and linens out and in boxes before they arrive. I want a couple of pictures in that room and that's all.

The lawyer for the estate had been kind enough to procure and stow moving boxes in the back mudroom. We spend the rest of the afternoon emptying cabinets of floral china and silver. Jared carries the now brimming boxes to the library, figuring we might as well store them there. We work well together. He passes me stuff, and I pack it. It's a good system because he can reach the stuff on the high shelves. This room takes considerably less time to go through than the library.

While I cook a simple meal of toast and canned soup, I putter around the kitchen. The only thing I have any interest in keeping is an old book of recipes. Flipping through its pages, I can't help but wonder which had been my father's favorites. Memories have a way of playing tricks on you. I wonder what memories my mind invented to make my dad seem more than what he was. It just doesn't seem possible that what I remember is real. No one's that perfect all the time.

I remember growing up on a farm or at least spending a lot of time on one. It wasn't in New England but somewhere further south, maybe Tennessee. Who knows?

Flashes of me climbing trees and working in a garden with my mom invade my thoughts. They were always smiling; could my mom and dad truly have been that happy all the time? It is safer not to trust those memories, nothing is ever that perfect. Or if that level of perfect existed maybe it tempted fate to destroy it. The risk versus reward of a so called happy ending scared me most of all. I've lived through having perfect, and then losing it.

"Three rooms down," I whisper a breath across my spoon to cool my soup.

Jared is intently shredding his toast into bits and pieces that cluster and float in his bowl. "How many more to go?"

I do the math in my head. "Three more down here, four upstairs, and I have no idea what's on the third floor."

"Want to check it out tonight?" He tilts his head to the side, almost as a dare.

"Do you think I'm scared?" I ask.

He shrugs. "Old house like this, that tower thing up there? It's got to be haunted."

I laugh and reply, "I ain't afraid of no ghost," in my best Ghostbusters impression.

He smiles. "I'll protect you from them either way."

Oh, is big bad Jared going to protect me from the things that go bump in the night? I want to argue, but I let him have this. I let him think he can.

After we rinse the bowls and put them in the dishwasher, we head up to the third floor. I'm not scared, mainly curious. I've never been up here before. A narrow set of stairs bloom from a skinny door opposite the second floor bathroom. That, with the steep slant of the steps, makes me immediately dismiss this floor as being used for anything other than storage. There is another narrow door at the top of the stairs.

I can imagine how claustrophobic it would feel to be on these stairs with both doors closed. There isn't even a light. Jared's using his cell phone to light the way, after insisting he go first. He has to give the top door a good shove, and it takes a minute for him to find the light switch. When he does, my mouth drops. We're in what must have been my father's room.

I turn, unsure of where to settle my gaze. When I had been here all those years ago, I had gone in search of his room and assumed my grandmother had just erased every trace of him. How wrong I was. This room had obviously been cared for. There's dust on flat surfaces but no more than the rest of the house.

"I think this was my dad's room," I quietly explain to Jared as he seems to be wondering why I'm just standing there.

He scratches the back of his head. "Do you want me to leave you alone?"

I shake my head and walk over to the twin-sized bed that's tucked under one of the sloping walls. I sit on it, tucking my feet under me and look around. My father may have sat in the same place and done the same thing.

My eyes fall on a door perpendicular to the wall of the door through which we entered. It hits me that this room is too small to represent the entire third floor.

I clear my throat and ask Jared if he wants to check it out, that it might be the entrance to the widow's walk. He hesitates but eventually nods and leaves me. I know I had, initially, wanted him to stay, but now I want to be alone in this space. There's a small wooden nightstand next to the bed. It's made of a warm toned wood, maybe maple. I gently tug the drawer open and pull it all the way out and set it on the bed next to me.

There isn't much in it. Some papers, mainly blank, others with notes that don't mean anything to me. There's some loose change and buttons. I pick up one of the buttons. It's small and metal with ivy leaves. I wonder what shirt or jacket it came from before dropping it back into the drawer and putting the drawer back into the nightstand.

My head pops up when Jared walks back into the room. "I found the stairs for the tower thing. Want to come see? It's pretty cool."

His crooked smile is infectious. I stand and cross the room to him, grasping his outstretched hand. The room off my father's room appears to have been used for storage, like an attic. There's a set of circular stairs even narrower than the ones leading from the second floor. Jared's hand tightens around mine as we follow the curved stairs upward. When we reach the top, it takes a moment for my eyes to adjust to the night sky.

My grandmother's house is by no means isolated, but there's some distance to her nearest neighbors. Still, the lights from the other houses on her street somehow give me comfort. I'm not sure why I'm uneasy. I'm not scared of heights or the dark or anything.

A window seat wraps around the small space, except for the opening for the stairs. Jared sits down, tugging me into his lap and burying his nose in my hair.

"How are you doing?" His words are hot against the back of my neck, the concern in them clear.

I shrug, sagging against him. I don't know how I am.

chapter 4 ½

Jared

I hate that she isn't letting me in. All I want to do is take care of her, but she's so fucking stubborn. Why does she have to do it all on her own? My hand rests on her hip, holding her as she leans against me. I can't help but wonder what she's thinking.

Sawyer is so small in comparison to me. When her eyelids start falling, I sit, easing her into my lap. She's almost asleep. I should probably wake her, let her walk down the stairs, and climb into bed. She would want that, to do it all by herself. Instead, I hold her in my arms until she falls all the way to sleep, her gentle snores letting me know when she's really gone.

She snuggles into me, her hands on my chest. She fits me, as though she was made to be in my arms. I've never felt this way with anyone else.

Any relationship I had before her now seems like practice before the real deal. A relationship test drive at the dealership until you sit in the right car and just know. It molds to your back making you sit up straighter and park in the back of the parking lot to protect it from any door dings.

I'd protect her the same way, keep her safe because somehow she molds to me in a way that makes me stand taller. Sawyer can push my buttons like no one else. I'm hardwired to her touch. She pushes me away and pulls me back all at the same time. I lean back farther against the back of the built-in window seat, looking out into the night.

Birch trees illuminated by a neighbor's house almost glow against the dark sky. The single-paned windows offer little resistance to the chill outside. If she keeps this place, they should be replaced. Some heavy-duty double-paned ones would be better. Maybe some foam insulation in the walls.

I shake my head, remembering it doesn't matter. It's too bad she's selling this place. I can picture her here, in this amazing house. My dad is all into family history. Maybe it's rubbing off on me now. I get why she doesn't want it. She has no personal attachment to this place.

She has no attachments anywhere.

chapter 5

Sawyer

I wake up in my bed the next morning and realize Jared must have carried me down those stairs. I'm surprised, considering how tight those stairwells are. It could not have been easy. He took the opportunity to sleep in my room, knowing if I was awake, I may have chased him away. His back is to me. I resist the urge to huddle up closer to him, and slip out of the bed instead.

After making myself some tea, I take it back upstairs, all the way up to my father's room. There's a small bookshelf next to a writing desk. It seems my father was a fan of Robert Frost. Leaning against the desk, I open the book to a random page and read a poem aloud.

There's a moment's pause at its end. Jared startles me by speaking, "Robert Frost?"

"How'd you know?" I ask, surprised. "I didn't know you were into poetry."

"Lucky guess," he shrugs. "I think he even had a farm somewhere in New Hampshire."

I close the book with a snap and set it on the desk behind me. "I didn't know that."

"That's a first," he says it like a joke, but the humor is missing from his tone.

"What's that supposed to mean?" I've never been one to back down.

He leans back against the doorjamb, and I worry about him slipping. "Simmer down, Sawyer. Just funny that I knew something you didn't."

I relax. "Come away from the stairs. You're making me nervous, and there's tons of stuff you know that I don't."

He looks over his shoulder and down the stairs with a smirk before moving further into the room. I wonder what he's thinking; hoping he isn't reading anything into my concern.

"Starting up here today?" His eyes are on the doorway to the widow's walk.

I ignore his question for now. "Let's check out the view now that it's light out."

He opens the door for me, and I try not to feel his eyes scorching my ass as I make my way up the curving stairs. The stairway is bathed in morning light. I make my way quickly to the top. I don't need an over-sized house in New England but part of me wonders what it would be like to sit on the ledge on a spring afternoon or a summer night so I can watch all the fireflies dance in the trees.

That won't happen though. With any luck, I'll be back in Denver, and this place will be long sold. It snowed overnight, not much, but enough to make the sunlight's reflection glaring. I keep my gaze off the ground and into the ice blue sky and cluster of birch trees behind the house. I'm usually never at a loss for words, but I feel tongue-tied. I want to spend the rest of our time here in my father's old room, but admitting that for some reason makes me feel weak so I hold it in instead.

After maybe thirty minutes, Jared breaks the silence. "Do you want me to look at the stuff in the side attic?"

I slump further into the window seat in a brief protest before nodding my response and following him back down the stairs. He gets straight to work, looking through boxes in the attic while I run downstairs and grab each of us two packs of mini muffins to eat while we work. Jared accepts his with a grunt, and I leave him.

Maybe an hour later, I get up to check on him when I hear him coughing. I stand frozen behind him when I realize the sound isn't from a cough but his attempt to disguise the fact that he's crying. I hesitate for a split second while I realize what's going on. This is my friend, my lover. I cannot ignore this.

I quietly sit down next to him and wrap my arms around his waist, ignoring his flinch at being caught. I'm about to ask him what's wrong when I see what he's holding in his hands. I painfully swallow the question on the tip of my tongue and press my face into his arm in an attempt to erase the image of his hands clutching a tiny-footed sleeper.

Is it awful that I know in that moment that this thing between us has to end? I don't ever want to have children, and Jared does, based on his reaction to a box of old baby clothes. He wipes his face and escapes my grasp, soon standing.

"I'm going to go clear my head," he says, glancing back at me before walking out of the attic.

With kids you lose your control, your individual ability to be responsible only for yourself. My parents were amazing but they still died. What if I ever had a kid and died too? I pick up the sleeper he was holding and gently place it back in the open box before putting the lid back on it. I go up to the widow's walk and call Sarah.

I can see his figure shuffling through the snow when she picks up.

"Hey, babe; how's everything going up there?" she asks.

I clear my throat, turning my head once he disappears from sight. "Jared just lost it going through some baby stuff in the attic."

I hear her gasp before she replies, "Oh, my God. That's awful."

I trail my finger down the glass leaving a mark. "I didn't know what to say. He left, went for a walk to think."

"What are you doing talking to me? Go find him."

"But he wants space." I cringe at how foreign those words sound.

She inhales loudly through her nose. "Sawyer Sterling, when have you ever respected someone's boundaries?"

She's right. "I don't know what to say to him."

Not knowing what to say never would have stopped me from getting all up in someone's shit before. Didn't stop me from pushing Will's mom and she lost not only a child but her spouse as well.

"Just find him and hug him. You don't have to say anything to him," she argues.

I agree and hang up on her, promising I'll call her later to let her know what happened. I trudge downstairs and start pulling on my boots when he walks in. His face is red from the wind. I hurl myself at him with more abandon then I actually feel. I'm not used to being scared so I decide to act like I'm not. Thankfully, his arms coil around me tightly, lifting me, leaving me no hope to pull away from him, because I would have pulled away from him.

His lips search for mine, ghosting a trail up my neck, across my chin before settling on mine. I'm unprepared for the emotion behind this kiss. There is an invitation in it that I can't accept, and he feels it. He releases me, gently setting me down before placing one chaste kiss on my forehead.

I sink back down to the bench by the door as he moves to lean against the wall facing me. It's coming. I can tell. I've been here before. We're going to have the "where is this going?" talk.

He examines his boots and the small puddle of melted snow forming around them before his eyes drift up to mine. "I'm in love with you, Sawyer."

I start to say something, but he stops me by lifting his hand. "And I know you don't love me back."

My mouth hangs open. I should say something. I should tell him that I do love him but that would be a lie because he isn't talking about the love you have for a friend. The love he wants from me I don't have to give. I'm just missing that piece.

"Jared…" My voice trails off.

He squats in front of me, cupping my face in his hands. "I knew what I was getting into with you. You don't have to love me back."

That's a first. This is usually where any guy I'm seeing and I will go our separate ways. I'm not prepared for him to say it's okay that I don't love him that way.

"I do love you," I insist.

"As a friend," he finishes the sentence I intended to leave unsaid.

His hands drop to his boots, untying one and then the other. He's still crouched right in front of me.

Once they're loose, he slides his hands up my legs to cup me behind my knees. "Right now, all I want to do is take you upstairs and bury myself in you. You game?"

I gulp as I nod, unable to find an adequate response for the hundredth time today. He pulls hard on my legs, pulling me into his lap as my hands rise to grip his shoulders. He stands, taking me with him. He steps out of his boots before carrying me upstairs. His mouth hovers in front of mine, but we don't kiss. Instead, our eyes stay locked in some sort of sensual staring contest. I don't know why, but I won't blink first, not now.

He sets me down on the edge of the bed and slowly peels my clothes off. As each layer is removed, I feel warmth instead of the chill I should. He's slow, methodical in his movements. It takes me a moment to grasp what's different. This isn't just sex. The expression in his eyes confirms it. His gentle touch erases any doubt.

Jared is about to make love to me.

I scoot back further onto the bed and watch as he slowly undresses. He climbs onto the bed and crawls up my body. He lies down next to me, turning me onto my side so that I'm facing him. He reaches up and strokes my cheek before leaning in and capturing my lips. I melt into his arms as the space between us disappears.

He's hard. I can feel the length of him pressing against me. I don't understand why he hasn't pushed himself inside me yet.

I reach for him, but he pushes my hand away.

"I'm not done kissing you," he explains against my lips.

"I can multitask," I argue, reaching for him again.

He leans back, away from me. "I know what you're trying to do, and it's not going to happen."

"What am I trying to do?" I ask, confused.

His hand moves to my shoulder, gently pushing me until I'm on my back. He answers me as he kisses, licks, and nips his way from my neck to my shoulder.

Softly, he reaches up to trace the outline of my phoenix tattoo, slowly following his fingertip with gentle kisses. He's marking me, on top of my ink. I had gotten this tattoo so long ago to symbolize rebirth, shedding my past to embrace my future. Here I was smack dab in the middle of my past with the man who clearly wanted my future.

He moves lower, his lips now teasing my pint-sized breasts. I can't ignore the phantom throb beating from each inch of skin he's touched.

"I know you like it hard and fast, but," he pauses to suck my nipple into his mouth, twirling his tongue around it before releasing, "have you ever let someone take their time with you?"

Never. It scares me. It feels like I'm losing control.

His hazel eyes seem to see right through me when he adds, "Just let me love you."

Before I can even think it through, I nod, and he continues lavishing attention to every single part of my body. What is so different about him? All thoughts evaporate as my body relishes his every touch. He continues to push my hands away when I try to touch him. He is in complete control of me. At first, it annoys me. I like being sexually aggressive. I'm most comfortable when I'm in the lead. I trust Jared, though, so I relax, allowing myself to just be.

He's relentless in his goal of pleasing me. As liberated as I am sexually, I always shied away from receiving oral sex. It just feels too intimate, someone's mouth directly on my sex. I cry out as my body quakes under his ministrations.

I've already come, but he continues, licking, flicking, and nipping at my already sensitive clit. His fingers gently twist inside me until my eyes roll back into my head again. I've balled the comforter up in each of my hands. I lift my head to look down at him as I pant. He looks up at me, and his expression terrifies me. It's a look of complete adoration. It's love. What scares me is I know I can't return it.

He slowly crawls up my body. I feel weighted, as though the signals from my brain to my limbs aren't firing, as they should. His lips on mine reawaken my slumbering limbs, and I lift my arms to wrap them around his neck. His cock slips into me. I'm too preoccupied by the delicious fullness of him that it takes me a moment to realize he never put on a condom.

This is the first time there is truly nothing between us. I pinch my eyes shut, as I will myself not to be affected. This doesn't change anything, even if it means more to Jared than it does to me. This is just sex.

He stills. "Sawyer?"

"Yes," I answer, my eyes still closed.

He settles down onto me, his hand coming up to cup my face. "Look at me."

His weight on me feels amazing, but his request unnerves me. "No."

His breath catches and whooshes back out as he asks. "Why won't you look at me?"

I turn my face into one of his hands. "I can't."

His breath is hot on my cheek as he leans down to kiss my cheek. I feel tears I don't understand behind my lids. Then he's gone, his weight, his fullness inside of me. He's pulled out, and now he's sitting just out of reach at the end of the bed, his head in his hands.

I peer at him for a moment, my gut twisting before crawling over to him.

He flinches when my fingertips graze his back. Before I can pull my hand away, he reaches for my hand and kisses it.

"Jared." I want to crawl into his lap, feel his arms around me.

Instead, he stands and avoids my eyes. "I think I should go home."

My mouth drops. "Because I wouldn't look at you?"

He shakes his head and turns to face me.

"I thought I could handle loving you even if you don't love me back." He traces the side of my face with his hand, his eyes dull, their usual spark extinguished.

"But I don't want you to go," I plead.

He swallows. "We don't always get what we want."

He doesn't say it with anger or malice but with regret and longing.

He pulls his clothes back on, and quietly leaves the room, as he lets me know he'll be on the computer downstairs checking flights. I get dressed, feeling emptier than I remember ever feeling before. Instead of going downstairs, I curl up in a ball on my bed and feel sorry for myself instead. Most girls would think I'm crazy. They would think Jared is a catch, and he is. He also deserves someone who can actually love him back. It just isn't me.

I get up when I hear my cell phone buzz. It's in the pocket of my jeans but must have fallen out and onto the floor while they were either coming off or being pulled back on. It's Sarah.

I lay back down, phone tucked under my ear. "Hey, babe," I fake happy.

"Oh honey, what's wrong?" she immediately asks, proving I fail at faking anything.

"Jared told me he loves me." I blink away inexplicable tears.

"Shouldn't that be a good thing?" she replies quietly.

"I don't love him," I argue, even though the words feel wrong.

"Are you sure about that?" she counters.

I get up and start pacing. "Yes, I'm sure." Am I, though? Am I one hundred percent certain I don't feel that way about him?

"If you say so," her singsong acquiesce stings. She goes on, "What happened after he told you?"

I pause by the window and lean my forehead against the pane. "He told me that he knew I didn't love him back, but he was okay with that."

"And?" she encourages me to go on after a long pause.

"He carried me upstairs and asked me to let him love me." I gulp when I hear her gasp on the other end.

"I tried, but I couldn't look at him, and he stopped and said it would be better if he went home." I wipe away a tear, not knowing why I'm crying.

"He's going back to Denver?"

I sniffle. "He's downstairs checking flights right now."

"Oh, honey." I hear her sigh.

"I'm fine," I lie. "I am."

"Do you want me to come up?"

I pinch the bridge of my nose. "Don't come up. I'm a big girl. I can handle this."

"I'm not saying you can't handle it." I can hear her frustration through the phone. "I'm just saying you're my best friend, and I love you and want to be there for you."

I look toward the door when I hear Jared clear his throat. He looks past me.

"Can I call you back?" I ask Sarah and hang up after she says okay.

Jared scratches the back of his head and looks away. "Would it be too weird to ask you for a ride to the airport? I can take a—"

I cut him off, "Please don't go."

He slowly crosses the room, pulls me tightly against him, and kisses the top of my head. "We both know I can't stay."

I bury my face in his chest and inhale. "That's not true."

"I just need some time to think about things. Being here with you will just be too hard. The last thing I want to do is lose you as a friend."

I look up at him. "You could never lose me."

He brushes some hair away from my eyes and smiles sadly down at me. Little crinkles tug the sides of his eyes. "You say that now."

I turn my head back toward the window and press my cheek to his chest. "I can't change your mind?"

"I need to go," he sighs.

I stiffen in his grasp, and he releases me, taking a step back. "How soon?"

He looks up at the ceiling. "I should pack now. Maybe in thirty minutes."

"That soon?" The hurt is evident in my voice. I had hoped he would at least stay the night.

"It was the only flight I could transfer my seat to," he explains.

I push past him. "I'll wait for you downstairs."

I don't hear his mumbled response as I hurry down the steps. I make it to the kitchen and use the countertop to hold myself up. What the hell just happened? It's like I'm losing my oldest and dearest friend.

I drink some water in an attempt to keep my throat from closing up. I feel betrayed. He asked me to let him love me, but when I can't immediately respond, he leaves me. My pain morphs into anger as he packs. When I hear the clump of his boots hitting the ground floor, I charge him.

"This whole thing is bullshit. You know that. That was real nice, Jar, asking me to open up and let you love me. Awesome that you loving me means you'll ditch me the second I do something you don't like."

His eyes widen, and he drops his duffle bag. "That's not fair."

"Fair?" I grumble. "You gave me all of five minutes to wrap my brain around the fact that you claim to love me." I point to his bag. "This doesn't fucking feel like love."

I'm not a person who shouts. I don't believe you need to yell to get your point across. Besides, it gives me a sore throat. Instead, I continue my rant in my normal volume. It unnerves Jared. I watch him rub his hands together before he just sinks to the steps behind him.

His eyes look haunted when they look up into mine. "I feel like an asshole leaving, but can't you see this is self-preservation?"

His question stops me cold. "What do you mean?"

He motions for me to come over to him, and against my better judgment, I do. I'm in his lap with his arms around me. It's so hard not to melt into him, but I'm angry so I deny myself that satisfaction.

"I fucked everything up, haven't I?" he says after some time.

"Only if you leave," I whisper.

"I'm scared to stay," he replies.

I feel like I'm talking sense into him, so I brush my lips across his neck and feel solace in the way he shivers at my touch.

I lift my hand to his chin and turn his face to mine. "I'll try if you stay."

I'm not even sure what I'm saying. I just don't want him to go.

"Okay." There is defeat in his reply.

It makes me wonder if I'm being selfish in asking him to stay.

chapter 5 ½

Jared

I'm never going to recover from her. She's going to chew me up and spit me out, and I'll be done. Why the fuck did I tell her I love her? I knew. I knew I couldn't push her, but I did it anyway. I felt like I was lying not saying it out loud. That every moment I wasn't telling her I loved her, I was betraying her.

I hold her until she stiffens, and then I drop my arms and let her go. If you love something…fuck. Is leaving the right thing to do? Or is staying going to be the thing that ruins this crazy thing we have going? She stands and steps away from me. Minutes go by before I get up. I make myself go somewhere in the house she isn't.

I go to our room and pull out my phone. I come close to calling my mom, but I don't want to worry her. It's just that seeing those baby clothes is still fucking with my head.

Would my baby have been a boy or girl? We never made it far enough into the pregnancy to find out. We buried Baby Keller. Now the word baby has morphed into the name of my child that never lived long enough for me to meet. Is there a heaven and if there is, will my baby have lived long enough here on earth for me to meet him or her there?

Did my baby die because I wasn't in love with Kristy but trying to be? I drag my hand over my face and wipe the tears from my eyes. I haven't even thought about the baby, my baby, in months.

I press her name without even thinking. "Hey, Kristy."

I can hear the surprise in her voice. "Jared, is everything okay?"

She's a nice girl. We were so wrong for each other but she is still a good person. "I came across some baby things, and it made me think about stuff."

"Oh, Jared, I'm so sorry. Do you want to talk about it?"

That's something that always drove me crazy about her. She always apologized for things, stuff that wasn't her fault. Why do girls do that? Why apologize for something you didn't do?

"It just hit me hard," I admit.

"I know what you mean. Sometimes that happens to me too. One second I'm fine, the next I'm crying."

"That's pretty much what happened."

"Oh, honey. Do you want me to come over?"

Shit. No. "I'm in New Hampshire. I should probably go."

"Okay, well, if you want to get together when you're back in town, just give me a call, okay?"

"Thanks. I'm not sure when I'll be back. I'll talk to you later."

I'm pretty sure my ex-wife just hit on me.

chapter 6

Sawyer

Over the next two days, we finish sorting through my father's room, the attic, and all of the rooms on the second floor. A moving van comes on the second day to pick up the dining room set for Sarah and Will. Jared and I are okay. We haven't had sex since I asked him to stay, but he is sleeping in my room at night. I've never been a cuddler before, but I seem to have no problem falling asleep in his arms each night.

When I wake the third morning, I notice I'm alone. Usually, I wake up before Jared. The bed feels cold without him. I roll over into his spot and lie on his pillow for a moment. I've become addicted to the way he smells. I get up after a couple minutes and go in search of him. He's in the kitchen, drinking a cup of tea.

"Can I make you a cup?" he asks when I walk into the room.

"Sure." I follow him to the stove and lean against him as he turns the burner on under the kettle.

We stay there and wait for the shrill cry of the kettle. Jared already has a mug set out for me. I guess I'm predictable that way. He adds water to my mug, and I move around him to add a teabag and some honey to it and stir it. I sit on the counter and take small sips of my tea while Jared moves to grab his mug and lean against the counter across from me.

"What's the plan for today?" he asks after finishing his.

"There isn't much left. I guess we hit my grandmother's room first and then maybe the living room."

"I'm going to grab a shower first." He rinses his mug and loads it into the dishwasher.

"Did you already eat?" I slide off the counter and grab myself a package of mini muffins.

He pauses to kiss the top of my head. "I did." Then he's gone.

I eat my muffins and finish my tea. I toy with the idea of joining him in the shower but I'm scared to make the first move. I'm just relieved he stayed and that he isn't being weird.

I wait until I hear the water cut off before I head upstairs to take my shower. Jared's standing in the bathroom, brushing his teeth, his towel wrapped precariously low around his waist. I feel pulled to him by a force I can't control. I stand behind him and kiss away lingering drops of water from his back. He stills, but I continue, my hands resting on his waist. He leans over to rinse his mouth before turning to face me.

Gentle hands cup my cheek as he lowers his minty lips to mine.

"I missed kissing you," I admit.

"I wouldn't have stopped you." He rests his head on top of mine.

My cheek scales The Rockies as I snuggle closer to him. "I came up to take a shower."

"If you were faster, you could have joined me in mine."

"I was trying to give you space." What I don't say is I was waiting for him to come to me.

"How'd that work out for you?" he asks, tightening his arms around me.

"I failed miserably." I turn my face to kiss his skin again.

He leans back to look down at me. "Don't think about it that way. Nothing that feels this right can be a failure."

"I can't argue that."

He cups my cheek with one hand as his mouth covers mine. His other hand grips me tightly to him. I mentally pause for a moment to wish I had at least brushed my teeth or showered. It doesn't stop me, though, not when Jared's urgent lips are on mine. He loves me, wants me any way I come. Knowing that still scares me. I feel responsible for his heart. No part of me wants to hurt him.

I have never wanted to love someone more in my life. I just don't know how. The responsibility of it, knowing he loves me, I have to be careful. This is brand new for me. Pushing love away is so instinctive for me, I worry I might even hurt him without being conscious I'm doing it.

It's impossible to be sensible when his lips and hands are on me. Ignoring my fears for now, I dive headfirst into the bliss he offers me. His towel is no match for the way our bodies move against each other. I giggle against his lips when it finally falls, leaving him naked and me still in my pajamas. He turns, lifts me onto the sink and moves his hands under my shirt. I lift my arms and break our kiss only long enough for the material to pass between us.

He grabs me by the back of the neck with one hand, and he kisses me again. His other hand dips into the front of my pants. I lift my legs to wrap around his waist, moaning into his mouth as his fingers find me.

"I want you," I argue.

"You have me," he teases.

"You know what I mean," I pant as his lips move downward, tracing my jaw before he latches onto one of my nipples.

"Fuck," I groan, leaning back against the mirror, one hand flying out and knocking over the toothpaste holder as I try to hold myself upright.

The nozzle of the sink digs into my back, but I ignore how uncomfortable I am when his fingers enter me. My other hand holds his head to my chest as he moves from one breast to the next. Two fingers rock in and out of me as his thumb rubs my clit. I am so fucking turned on it doesn't take long for that pressure to start building inside of me. I start begging for his cock, wanting to feel him explode inside of me. He laughs, promising I'll get it before he bites down on my nipple.

My eyes roll back as I tighten around him, my whole body pulsing with pleasure.

He pulls his hands out of my pants and moves to lift me, freezing when he sees my back in the mirror. "Shit, Sawyer."

I turn my head and watch his fingers dust the angry red grooves the faucet left from biting into my skin.

His eyes move to meet mine in the mirror. "Did I hurt you?"

I shake my head, reaching around to touch my back. I regret it when I wince. That's going to leave a mark.

It serves as a definite mood killer for him, though. He gently lifts me, his hands are under me, my arms are around his neck, and he carries me to my room.

"I'm fine," I insist as he softly sets me down.

He gives me a stern look. "I'm getting some ice."

I ease myself onto my side and watch a still very naked Jared leave the room. Not fair, damn faucet. I could be having sex right now. I reach around to touch it again. It feels like a giant bruise brewing.

Jared comes back with some ice in a sandwich bag wrapped in a couple paper towels.

He lies down in front of me, facing me, and holds the bag to my back. He only stops, to grab a blanket to cover us both.

"What am I going to do with you?" he asks, giving me a chaste kiss.

I grin. "I can think of a couple things."

He frowns, not amused. "Why didn't you tell me I was hurting you?"

I put my hand on his chin, making sure he's looking me in the eyes. "I didn't feel a thing during, I swear."

It's his turn to grin. "Didn't feel a thing?"

I push at his chest. "You know what I meant."

The chill from the ice has numbed my back, but the blanket Jared grabbed isn't keeping the chill from spreading. I shiver, and he shifts closer to me, the warmth from his naked body heating me. I rub my nose up and down on his neck and laugh when he starts shaking and goes almost rigid. I stop.

"Are you ticklish?" I gasp.

"Don't," he warns, failing to deny it.

My momentary excitement over learning this is paused by another violent shiver. "Can we take the ice off?" I plead.

He lifts the blanket and moves the ice from my back to look at it before nodding and setting the bag on the floor behind him. When he straightens back up, he pulls the blanket back over us and tugs me into his arms.

"I'm sorry," he whispers against my forehead.

"Stop that," I snap. "It wasn't like you did it on purpose. Plus, I know what'll take my mind off my back being sore." I halfheartedly attempt, knowing my odds of getting laid in my current perceived injured state is unlikely.

He takes the bait, though. "And what's that?"

I grin up at him, hopeful. "You."

He tucks a strand of hair behind my ear. "You got me."

"That's not what I meant," I groan, knowing that probably came out wrong.

I know by the hurt expression he quickly masks.

I move my lips to his neck and slip one hand between us to stroke his cock. I hope that my actions will speak for me and smile as I feel him harden under my attention.

I wiggle out of my pants, and he doesn't fight me when I push him until he lays flat on his back. The now unnecessary blanket slips from my shoulders and pools behind me as I straddle him.

"Are you sure?" he says, unable to disguise the want in his voice.

I wrap my fingers around him and slide them up and down his length, loving the way he hardens even more under my touch. I shift my weight onto my knees and position him under me before slowly easing down until he fills me. We groan together. I've missed this the last two days.

I lean down to kiss him as his hands coast up my legs to grip my ass. He grinds his hips against mine, and I feel every delicious inch of him inside me. I start to pull back to start my ride but still when he bites my lip. My eyes open and lock on to his as he releases my lip and slides his tongue over the place his teeth bit into me.

"Stay right there," he orders, his hands circling around my waist.

He slowly lifts me, holding me up for a moment before pulling me down hard as he thrusts his hips up to meet me. I grip his biceps as he repeats this move over and over again, throwing my head back every time he slams into me. He sits up suddenly, my body moving with him. We're both sitting now, face to face, our mouths only a breath apart. He still lifts and lowers me, only slower now. My hands slide up to rest on his shoulders.

I watch his eyes as he makes love to me. They tell me so much more than I already know. His eyes are like one of those trick pictures at the mall that you stare and stare at, trying to see the hidden picture. When you tilt your head just so and relax your eyes, when you just stop trying so hard, the image is revealed. In his unguarded eyes, I see how scared he is, but hopeful at the same time.

For me, it's a responsibility I'm not ready for. The power he wields over my body is not as stubborn as that of my heart.

I come hard, vibrations echo throughout my limbs as my eyes close. Jared follows me, unable to withstand the pleasure of my body pulsing around him. Our first time without a condom adds an unexpected thrill when I feel him release inside me.

I open my eyes to his and open my mouth knowing I'll probably say something stupid and somehow ruin this moment. He must know it too because his lips silence any words that might come out of mine. He leans me back down on my side and leaves me, his warmth quickly replaced by the chill in the room as I watch him walk out of the room.

He returns after just a moment, a washcloth in his hand. I watch, as he wipes off the inside of my thighs. I have never dated a guy who has done that. It's so strangely intimate.

"You don't have-" I move to get up, but he stops me.

"Let me." He pauses, his hand hovering over me.

I relax back onto the pillow and let him take care of me. It feels foreign, letting someone take care of me. The caregiver is a role I have always sought out myself. I took care of Sarah when she was getting over Will. I took care of Will's mom so he and Sarah could have a shot at being together again. This is new for me. He must sense my tension and shifts up to kiss my forehead before taking the washcloth back to the bathroom.

He comes back into the room, shifting me over so there is room to lie beside me. "I could live inside you," he murmurs against the top of my head, "all day and all night for the rest of my life."

I don't say anything, but for the first time in my life, I imagine spending it with someone.

After a comfortable snuggle, we convince ourselves to get up and out of bed before we end up spending the day there. If we didn't need to finish going through the house, I would consider it. Plus, I'm hungry.

After getting dressed, Jared heads straight to the kitchen to make us sandwiches while I go to my grandmother's room. When I had stayed here, all those years ago, her room had been on the second floor. She must have moved it to the first floor so she wouldn't have to deal with the stairs anymore.

It's overcast outside, and even though it's barely lunchtime, opening the curtains is not enough to dispel the gloom. I turn on the lamps on either side of her bed and the lamp across the room sitting atop her dresser. Her lamps surprise me. They seem almost whimsical and don't fit the image of her that resides in my memories.

She had been cold, formal, and distant during those days. I was so young and had just lost both of my parents. I don't remember her even attempting to comfort me. I remember more compassion from the social worker that drove me to the airport than from her.

I start with her wardrobe. Since this room is a converted den, there wasn't a traditional closet in it, just a tall, oversized wooden wardrobe in one corner. It's brimming with your standard New England fashions: L.L. Bean cardigans in fall colors, turtlenecks, and long woolen skirts.

Jared clears his throat when he walks in the room. I turn and watch as he crosses the room and sets a tray of food on a table in front of one of the windows.

"Ham or turkey?" he asks as I sink into a chair next to the table.

"Turkey sounds good, unless you wanted that," I reply.

He turns the tray so the plate with the turkey sandwich is closer to me. I'm too hungry to wait for him and start while he pulls the bench at the end of her bed over to use as his seat.

I like watching him eat, always have. He always takes two bites and then a gulp of whatever he's drinking, without fail. He looks around the room as he eats, and my eyes follow his eyes' path. Other than the first day we were here, this is the first time we've been in this room, and even then, that first day all we did was open the door and peek inside. Both of Jared's grandmothers are still living. I wonder if this room reminds him of them.

"Is it weird?" he asks after one bite and taking his second while he waits for me to answer.

My eyes sweep the room before settling on his. "I feel like I shouldn't be here, like someone who knew her and cared about her should be going through her things."

"You should have asked that lawyer dude to do it."

I shake my head. "I thought," I gulp down the disappointment that threatens before going on, "maybe I'd find more stuff that belonged to my parents."

He reaches across the table to squeeze my shoulder.

I nod glumly. "Silver lining: Sarah and Will got a free dining room set."

"And," he smiles, "gotta admit that widow's walk is pretty sweet."

"It is a cool house," I agree. "I just wish I felt—" I shake my hands, trying to figure out want I want to say. "I wish I felt like I belonged here somehow, like there's something tying me here. It just feels like some stranger's house."

His eyes are soft pools of concern. I hurry to finish my sandwich and brush the crumbs off my pants to avoid his worried looks. Once I'm done, I go to her dresser because that part of the room is where my back will be toward him. I hear him quietly finish his lunch behind me.

There's a small TV off to one side of her bed. I consider turning it on to discourage any more talking, but I don't because I'd have to walk past him, and I'm pretty sure he'd try and hug me. I open and shut the first drawer loudly when I see it's full of old-lady underwear. It didn't cross my mind that I would be sorting hers.

"Everything okay?" he asks.

I wave at the wall in front of me. "Just old-lady panties."

His chuckle makes my cheeks redden, and I'm relieved he can't see my reaction. I ease the drawer open again. My plan is to take anything that isn't clothes out and set on top of the dresser. Any clothes can be boxed and donated. My fingers brush across the velvet top of a small jewelry box. I pull it out, snapping it open to inspect its contents. A small emerald ring winks back at me. It's simple, pretty. I cave to the impulse to try it on.

"Hey, Sawyer."

My head turns from admiring the ring on my finger to Jared as he holds up some papers.

"I think you should take a look at these," he continues.

I start to take the ring off but stop when it refuses to breach my knuckle. "What is it?" I ask, crossing the room.

He had made three piles on her bed from items that must have come from the deep drawer of her bedside table.

"Did you live on a farm?" He holds up a picture of me with my parents.

I gasp, reaching for it. The same day they died, I was picked up by a social worker and didn't have a chance to take anything with me, not that we had much. I hold the picture inches from my face in an effort to zoom in on the facial features of the two people who had brought me into this world. It had been so long that I had forgotten what they looked like. The sudden warmth and weight of Jared's hand on my shoulder forces my eyes up to his.

"Are those——?"

I finish his question for him, my eyes racing back to their smiles, "My parents."

I sink down to the floor, turning as my body nears it so my back rests against the side of her bed. The multicolored, braided rug beneath me offers little cushion.

The focus of the photo is us, my parents and I. We're standing in front of a small red tractor. My blonde braids brush my shoulders. My mom and dad crouch down on either side of me, my mom's hands gripping my waist. We smile in what looks like a happy, carefree way. I flip the photo over, my mouth drying at the revelation of script on the back.

Me and my girls, it read in what must be my father's hand.

The date stamping imbedded is the year I turned nine. "Are there more?" I ask, flipping the picture back over, my eyes not leaving their faces.

The bed is pushed back a breath under Jared's weight when he sits next to me. His hands are full of paper memories. We separate them into three piles: photos, letters and other paper documents, and the third pile is a leather bound journal. The smallest pile is of the photos. I decide to save that pile for last, wanting to dwell at length over each picture.

The largest pile is of all of the miscellaneous papers and letters she had saved. It overwhelms me so I start with the leather bound journal. Any expectation for flowery script or insight into who she is dies on the first page. Each entry reads like a checklist. Her first entry is dated 5.12.1984

5.12.1984

Late frost in the forecast. Put covers over the front flowerbeds. Got a letter from Henry. He will not be coming home this summer. Georgia Ramsey passed away. Sent flowers with card.

Each page is a laundry list-type step into the past. There are brief mentions of my mother early on. One entry, dated 12.16.1985, reads that she's coming with my father to her house for Christmas. Another one, just after Christmas, reads what my parents had given her as a present: a sweater and an engagement announcement.

Each entry is devoid of emotion. There's no reaction or personal investment from her in these entries. There are births, including my own, and deaths. These entries could have been a grocery list. An entry, dated 4.27.1992 documents our move to the farm.

chapter 6 ½

Jared

I watch as her fingers trace over each entry in the journal. It's as if a switch flips inside her. She's subdued, pensive, sitting right in front of me but somehow miles away. Sawyer's vulnerable.

All I want to do is to help her, be there for her. Instead, all I can do is quietly watch her deal with this on her own. This is Sawyer 101, and I hate it. This is when I feel like I'm walking on eggshells. One wrong word or move, and she'll pull away.

I'm here, but she's inside her head. I wish she would open up, vent, scream, or something. I know it bothers her that she never lived with her grandmother. I just don't understand why it bothers her so much. Her grandmother was one person, and if she didn't want Sawyer, she was an asshole. Plus, doesn't Sawyer get that if she had grown up here; there might have been a chance we never would have met?

Does that even matter to her? Sure, her grandmother sucked. Sure, having to live with strangers wasn't ideal, but it's not as if she had to go to a foster home or something. It's not like her grandmother completely relinquished custody of her. Who knows what might have happened to her if that had happened.

We not only may have never met, but she could have ended up some place a whole lot more fucked up than that school in Canada. I know a kid from work who grew up in foster care. He didn't get adopted until he was almost seventeen. He won't talk about it, but I know he saw some fucked up shit growing up.

Can't she just be happy that nothing like that ever happened to her? You can't dwell. You can't let this stuff make your life decisions for you. Bad stuff happens to everyone. There isn't much we can do to control it. All you can do is live with the bad and try to relish the good.

I want her to admit what she has is good. That she deserves more good in life. We both do. Someday, maybe just our being together will be the start of good things for the both of us. In the end that's all you can hope for, more good than bad. She just seems so far away. I don't know how to reach her without pushing her even further away from me.

chapter 7

Sawyer

My earliest memories are of working on a farm. My parents had been free spirits. Our work on the farm hadn't been manual labor in the sense of it being forced. It had been my parents' choice.

The farm's address is listed. I had known the farm was somewhere in Tennessee. Time had erased any other memories I had of its location. I can still remember the fields and orchard. We had apple, pear, and peach trees, not many, maybe ten of each. There were also fruit and vegetable gardens. We had some livestock, chickens for eggs, cows for milk, sheep for wool.

I used to joke that I had a free-range childhood, but in truth, I had. I was expected to help but still had plenty of free time to climb trees and play in the fields.

Hearing Jared clear his throat brings me back. I close her journal with a snap and lean my head back against the side of her bed, its wooden frame digging into my back.

"You okay?" His hand feels heavy on my knee.

I tilt my head to look at him. "You remember I lived on a farm. Before my parents died?"

I go on, "I was just thinking about it, the farm. I couldn't remember the name of the town it was in." I lift her journal. "It's in here, the address. I wonder if it's still even there."

"Would you ever want to go back?"

I lift my shoulder. "Maybe."

I look down again, opening her journal. I'm looking for one day in particular, 6.14.1997. The day my parents died. I'm not sure why I assume her entry that day will be different from any of the day's prior. It reads:

6.14.1997

Hendersons out of town. Fed cat, watered plants.

Reading Handmaiden's Tale, due to library 6.22,

Call from farm. Henry and Abigail died in a plane

crash. Sawyer coming 6.16. Make arrangements.

I hold the page open for Jared to read. "The day my parents died."

"They died in a plane crash? I don't think I knew that."

I stand, brushing nonexistent dust from my backside. "There was a small plane. I think my dad and another man flew it. They would take food and stuff from the farm places."

"Did you ever go with them?" He gets up too.

He's standing too close to me not to be touching me. I take a step away from him. "Sometimes, if they weren't going far."

I couldn't remember where they had been going, only that they had left so early that I was still asleep when they left. I didn't get to say goodbye, only goodnight when they had tucked me in the night before. Beau's parents didn't learn they had crashed until sometime after lunch. I had been in the orchard.

"Did they go far that day?"

I ignore his question and take another step away. "I had a kitten."

He was black with white paws.

"Boots."

I lift my head, my eyes darting to his. "How did you know?"

He reaches out his hand, mine lifting as well to meet it before he pulls me into his arms. "On the boat. I remember you talked about him."

"He had white paws."

We leave the pile of pages and documents we still need to go through. We leave the room, the journal, and the photos. We walk out into the kitchen. He leads me to a stool, helping me sit before going to put water on the stove. He pulls out two mugs and sets the teabags in them as he waits for the water to heat.

The ring I had forgotten about earlier is now causing a thumping pulse in my finger. I twist and pull, trying to work it over my knuckle but doing nothing other than rubbing a layer of skin from it.

"Give me your hand," Jared says, bringing over a bowl of soapy water.

Warm water slides over my digits, his hand holding mine. Under the water, the fingers of his other hand turn the ring, freeing my finger from its grasp. Both of his hands hold mine, the sweetness of the moment only broken by the shrill cry of the kettle behind us.

He leaves, setting the ring on the counter before going to move the kettle to a different burner and grab a dishcloth to dry our hands. He takes the dishcloth, which is still damp from his own hands, and he dries mine. Then he leaves to make our tea.

"What the fuck was up with her journal?"

He jumps. I had been quiet for so long I wonder if I scared him.

"Who writes a journal like a grocery list?" My voice rises with each word. "There were like three entries on each page, six if you count the backs." Dismissing the burn, my fingers curl around the mug he sets in front of me. "I don't hate people, but I think I hate her."

The gulp of tea I take after admitting that burns going down. His hand draws lazy figure eight patterns on my back. I lean toward him, comforted that he doesn't argue about what I said, just accepts it.

"What I don't get," I straighten back up, and he drops his hand, "are how many friends she had. Tons of people, all ready to watch me so she wouldn't have to."

"If she didn't have all of those friends, there's a chance we never would have met."

I turn to angle my entire body in his direction, contemplating a life not knowing him. "Nah, I have a feeling we would have met no matter what."

He lifts his mug to his lips and pauses before he drinks. "We'll never know." His other hand finds its way to my knee.

"What are we even doing here?"

Jared sets his drink back down as he cocks a brow at me. "Is that an actual question or—"

I hit his shoulder and can't suppress my own smile when I see his. "I know what we're doing here, but why are we doing it? What qualification do I have, other than being a blood relative, to sort through her things?"

"Then let's jam."

I use my drink as a reason not to immediately reply while I think it over. I can see an odd reflection of myself in the gloss at the bottom of the now empty mug. I put the cup back down.

"I want to go home."

Jared shifts me into his lap. "Then let's go home."

I email my grandmother's lawyer to arrange for the items I had stored in the breakfast room to be shipped to Denver. Even though I wasn't sure I wanted them, Jared makes sure everything from her nightstand comes with us: the pictures, documents, and my grandmother's journal. Then I book the next flight for us home.

Jared doesn't argue my driving the rental back to the airport. It's as though he knows I need to feel like I'm in control.

"Have you ever seen so much road kill?" I ask just to say something.

"Raccoons get run over in Colorado, too." He voice is lighter than his grip on the side handle.

"I've just never seen as many. Think they're suicidal here?" He sucks in a breath as I ride the bumper of the hatchback in front of us.

"Maybe there's a rogue Kool-Aid-drinking cult of them."

I ease back into my seat and off the bumper of the car in front of me. If Jared can joke with me, it means we're good. I need us to be good, not to be changed by whatever happened in New Hampshire.

Other than constantly asking if I'm okay, which I am, he doesn't seem to believe our leaving New Hampshire isn't a big deal. Jared sleeps, or pretends to sleep while I drive home from the airport. I think he's pretending because his body hardly moves when I switch lanes. Once we're back at the condo, he runs to the store to restock on food after we get our bags in.

I'm asleep on the sofa when he gets back. I wake in his arms as he carries me to my room. He cradles me against his chest, and I lean up to kiss his neck. When he looks down at me, I move my lips to his. If he's hesitant because I might be tired, it doesn't last long. His urgency grows with mine. I want to escape and get lost in him.

I don't complain when he stays in my room that night, having grown comfortable sleeping with him while we were away. The next morning, he wakes up before I do, pressing a hurried kiss to my forehead before racing off to work. The mountain waits for no one, I think to myself as I drift back to sleep.

When I finally wake up, I sink into a state of not knowing what to do with myself. I go through the motions. I shower; I eat a chocolate chip Eggo. I call the foreman in charge of the studio renovations and leave a lame message to check in. I call Sarah and rap Beastie Boys on her voicemail because she doesn't answer either.

Being alone is scary. I don't need to dwell on the negative. I need a distraction. After loading the washer up, I hop into my Hummer and go to the mall. Since my eighteenth birthday, I've never really needed to work for a living. I'm the sole beneficiary of a living trust in my name created by my parents before they died. I'm not a bajillionaire or anything, but with the exception of some first class airplane tickets, I don't spend a whole lot.

I had invested in Sarah's company, but she paid me back ages ago and then some. There's the condo and my Hummer, but it's not as if I bought a mansion and drive a Bentley. I like consignment stores for clothes and yoga instead of partying. I do have a few expensive pairs of shoes, but I'm short and they were purchased under the misguided assumption that if they cost more they might be comfortable. They aren't.

I get a chai latte and wander around the mall. I love to check out the kiosks in the middle of the walkways. The knockoff purses, the jeweled cellphone cases and the next miracle skin cream are always fun. You can tell the people who work them are on commission because they put used car salesmen to shame with their pitches.

I am sucked in by the girl with the magic hair straighter and am in her chair, heated wand to my scalp before I know it. The string-eyebrow-remover woman has her eye on me too. I'm curious about a straighter though, since my hair can get frizzy. After buying one, I dashed into the toy store across the way to avoid the eyebrow woman.

I amble up and down the aisles, thinking back to when I was small. My toys on the farm growing up were trees, kittens, and wide-open spaces. We didn't have a TV, just a radio. I grew up playing cards and checkers, not Mario Cart. After the summer I spent with Jared and his mom, I went to a boarding school in Canada. The headmistress was an Italian woman named Carmen Bartonili.

She knew my grandmother and took me in like her own. When I was thirteen, I saw the movie The Little Princess with Shirley Temple. I used to pretend that the news of my parents' deaths was a mistake, and they were in a hospital somewhere with bandages wrapped around their faces so nobody knew who they were. They would moan and mumble like the father in the movie for their little girl.

Carmen wasn't anything like the mean woman in the movie, though. She tried her best, but I think I missed Jared and the foreignness of being on a boat in the middle of the ocean too much to fit in there. On impulse, I buy a Tech Deck skateboard and avoid the eyebrow woman as I make my way back to my car.

Sarah calls me back right as I'm pulling in.

"Sabotage? Really?" Her hello.

I snort, "A classic."

"I'm not disputing this, only trying to figure out why I had a three minute serenade on my voicemail. FYI, I saved it and plan on playing it for Will when he gets home."

I kick-shut my door because my hands are full and wink at the mailman who stops to check out my car. "Whatever floats your boat, babe."

"So, how goes it?"

I can hear her fingertips moving across her keyboard and know she's multitasking. That girl is a workaholic. I make a mental note to remind Will to make her unplug before I answer. "We're back home. There's going to be an estate sale and whatever doesn't sell is going to be donated to the local woman's shelter."

"Oh." I fumble my keys at her exclamation. "We got the dining room set. I love it."

"Sweet. No scratches or anything from the move?" I chuck my now empty latte cup and take the bag from the toy store into my room, opening it as she answers.

"Nope, not a scratch on it and it fits perfectly in the dining room. We still need to get a rug to go under it. I tried to send Will out for it last night, but he refused to go without me."

I pull out a pair of nail clippers to bite into the plastic wrapping of the toy skateboard. "Um, can't say that I blame him. You can be hard to shop for."

"I am not," she argues.

I let it go, knowing better. My skateboard comes with two extra decks in case I want to change it out.

"How are things with Jared?"

I hedge, "What do you mean?"

"Don't pull that crap with me, Sawyer. This is the first time you've lived with someone you're," she pauses, "being intimate with. This is a big step for you, and I just wanted—"

"A big step?" I cut her off, questioning her choice of words. "Let's not get ahead of ourselves. Jared and I are just friends." I leave out the fact that she knows he loves me since that would hurt my argument.

"If you say so."

My mouth drops. That little... "I do say so. Nothing has changed. We're friends."

"Okay, sweetie."

Something in her tone makes me want to kick her. I'm interrupted, though, by my foreman calling on the other line. "I gotta hop, but I'm serious."

"All right, babe. Talk later." That's the last thing I hear before I click over.

The renovation had hit a snag that may put us a week back from the originally planned opening. It sucks but isn't the end of the world. We talk a bit longer, and I let him know I'll be stopping by the next day to check out the progress in person.

I'm switching another load of laundry into the dryer a few hours later when Jared walks in.

"Are you gonna make it?" I ask.

He looks like he had his ass handed to him.

"I think I'm getting old. I'm going to be hurting tomorrow." He lets his coat fall to the floor. He glances back at it as if he's contemplating picking it up before just deciding to leave it there.

"Tomorrow," I scoff. "You look like you're hurting right now."

He gives me a glum nod in assent, and I laugh at how pitiful he is in a cute way. "Want me to run you a bath?"

He's quick to reply, "Only if you'll join me."

I fill my tub with hot, bubbly water and climb in first so he lies in front of me. With his back to my chest, I do my best to rub the tension gathered in and around his shoulder blades. Before too long, he's asleep. I let him nap until the water starts to get cold and then make him get out. Only after I have him settled in my bed do I wonder why I didn't make him go to his own room.

He fights me, but I get him to eat some soup before he passes out again from exhaustion. I forget how strenuous his job is. When he doesn't take breaks and is used to it, the strain doesn't seem to affect him that much. I wonder what he'll do when he gets older. He won't be able to snowboard forever. Even though it's early, I curl up with him and drift off to sleep.

When I wake up, snuggled up to a deliciously shirtless Jared, I remember the Tech Deck I bought at the store. I ease out of his arms and grab the package from where I tucked it beside the bed. I carefully open the plastic encasing my new board so that I don't wake Jared.

His chest piece is mainly black and white, with every shade of gray between. There are subtle pale blue highlights at each peak of the snowcapped range. I'm gently sliding my board over his pecs on my second downhill pass when he shifts. Avalanche, I think to myself, as my board falls to the bed between us.

"What are you doing?" he asks with only one eye slightly open.

I retrieve my board and start again at the peak closest to me. "I'm snowboarding."

He shifts in bed so he's on his side facing me. He rubs sleep from his eyes and blinks a few times before watching the progression of my board across his chest.

"I've wanted to do this as long as you've had this tattoo," I admit.

"You've always wanted to fingerboard a skateboard across my chest?" he clarifies, still waking up.

I lift the deck from his chest, holding it up for him to see. "No wheels, so this is clearly a snowboard."

He doesn't argue my logic, and I return to my play, shivering when his fingertips crawl up my arm. "Do I get a turn? I think you have a better mountain range."

"Aren't you funny?" I tease, tossing my board and dropping my lips to his.

The bath last night must have helped because when Jared leaves this morning to do some actual snowboarding, he barely limps. Meanwhile, I'm heading over to the studio to talk with John, my foreman. One thing I like about the space is how close it is to my condo, maybe a fifteen-minute drive.

The front door is locked, and after banging on it loudly for a second time, John comes to open it.

"Sorry about that. It's hard to hear anything over the noise."

"Fair enough." I glance around. "The place looks great."

John's eyes follow mine. The walls are done and painted in the main room.

I shrug out of my coat, resting it over a stack of boxes, and cross my arms over my chest. "So what's the reason for the delay you mentioned on the phone?"

I've never been one to bullshit, and from what I've seen of John, he's the same way. He motions me to follow him over to another stack of boxes across the room. Opening the top, he pulls a strip of wood laminate out.

"They sent the wrong flooring and aren't able to get the right stuff out for," he pauses to gauge my expression, "at least another week."

My jaw drops. "At least? What's the worst case scenario?"

He pushes the plank back into the box and rubs his hand over his face. "Conservatively, I don't think they'll get it to us in a week. I think we're looking at closer to two weeks and then installation time."

I groan. This is not good news.

Looking back up at him, I ask, "There's no way we can use what they sent?"

He reaches down to pull the plank back out. "It's not the color you ordered."

It's almost an onyx-toned wood, the exact opposite of what I wanted. I wanted the place to feel light, airy, peaceful.

I shake my head. "You're right. That color is all wrong. I'm just annoyed. This is definitely gonna delay the opening day." I glance around again. "Does this throw other work off schedule too?"

"We can work around it. Once the floors are done, we should be done with everything else."

"Cool," I exhale and let John show me around.

Now that the walls are redone and painted, it's easier to envision the final space. The main entrance will open to a front desk type waiting area. This will be where people can check the calendar and sign up for classes or spa stuff. There is a short hallway with bathrooms, a room for facials, one for massages, and then a big open space for the yoga classes.

"I love it," I say to no one in particular.

Past the main yoga space, there is an office, storage room, and small locker room where people can lock up their coats and purses during class. John is standing back a ways, just watching me check out the place. I like him. He reminds me of myself. If I hadn't have been so busy, I might have asked him out when I hired him. He's a good-looking man in that faded jeans, tight white t-shirt way. I think he's single. I stop thinking about the studio and start thinking about which one of my friends I can set him up with.

"Are you single?" I blurt.

He blinks a couple times, and then grins, "Interested?"

I roll my eyes and laugh. "Not for me."

He shrugs. "That's too bad. It's been fun working with you."

"I'm a pain in the ass. Trust me. I have single friends, though."

"I'm probably a pain in the ass too. I don't have much free time these days to date."

"Well," I grin, "if you ever need a date…"

"I'll keep that in mind," He's grinning too.

I head home not long after. I'm just in the door when my grandmother's executor calls. The estate sale had been successful and anything that had not sold has already been taken to the shelter for donation. The house will officially go on the market tomorrow, but two realtors have already contacted him with buyers that are interested. The house is well known in town, so it should sell quickly. The tax hit will suck, but after that is set aside, the remaining money can just be deposited into my trust account.

It feels weird taking money from her. Part of me wants just to donate it all to charity. Speaking of charity, her executor asks if I'd like to continue the annual donation to the Hamilton Farm. I have no idea what that is, so after I look into it, I'll let him know what I plan to do going forward.

He asks me again what to do with her remains. I make some excuse about needing to go. It isn't a lie. I do need to send some emails, but they aren't anything urgent enough that I would have to hang up. After we hang up, I send emails to Catherine and Sheila to let them know the opening will be delayed. Both of them currently work out of their homes so it's not as if it's a giant impact to either of them, which makes me feel better.

I'm on my mat going through some relaxation poses when Jared gets home.

"That's a nice view."

I laugh, dropping my pose and ass to the floor.

"Aw, I shouldn't have said anything," he says, taking off his coat.

"Hush." I kneel next to my mat and roll it up. "Still as sore today?" I ask, standing.

He flops down onto the sofa. "Not as bad as yesterday."

"Sweet." I crawl into his lap and kiss him.

Is it possible for someone to smell like snow? I wonder to myself as I pull his earlobe between my teeth. He grinds his hips against mine. His hands are hot on my waist as he presses my body closer to his. As we kiss, we talk. I tell him about the delays to the studio. He tells me how the lifts malfunctioned halfway through the day, leaving skiers and snowboarders dangling while they fixed them.

Somehow, with his lips on my skin, I don't care about anything else. None of it matters. It's when he mentions his mom's in town and wants to have dinner with us that I pull away.

"What's wrong?" he asks. I'm now across the room and not in his arms.

"Did you say anything to her about us?" I ask.

His eyes widen. "Yes. Is that wrong?"

I start pacing. "Of course it is. What did you tell her? Why didn't you talk to me about it first?"

His knee bounces as his leg shakes. "I told her I'm in love with you."

My shoulders sag. "Why would you do that?"

He runs the tip of his tongue across the underside of his teeth before rubbing his lips together. "Are you angry at me because I told my mom how I feel about you?"

I look away. "I just wish we would have talked about what we were going to say to people first."

He stands and walks toward me before he changes his mind and walks to the kitchen instead. He opens the fridge, pours himself a glass of water, and drinks about half of it before looking back at me.

"What would you want me to call us, Sawyer?"

I shake my head. "I don't know."

He looks up at the ceiling, making me miss his hazel eyes. "I don't know what else to do. I feel like you're pushing me away." He lowers his head, eyes locking on mine. "Are you pushing me away?"

I nod, unable to lie to him.

He looks back at the ceiling, and I can't help but follow his gaze, wondering if there are answers somewhere up there.

When he looks back down, he keeps his eyes on the glass in his hands and not on me. "Why are you pushing me away?"

This time, I do walk over to him. I take his glass from him and set it on the counter. I fold his arms around me. "I don't know how to do this."

"We don't have to do anything, Sawyer. We can just be together."

"It's not that easy. I don't know why it bothers me that your mom knows. It just does."

His arms relax around me. "Are you tired of me?"

I head-butt his chest. "Don't be a dumbass."

chapter 7 ½

Jared

This is progress. She didn't run. She could have. She could have walked right out that door and out of my life. I wrap my arms around her and lift her. Any residual soreness is forgotten. Her skin is the only balm I need. I probably should have talked to her before I outed us to my mom.

Thank fuck it worked, though. It feels like another step. A step to her admitting there is something here. If people know, maybe she will be less likely to bail. I'll take all the help I can get. Besides, my mom is like slow pitch softball, a bunny hill. She knows Sawyer and already loves her.

I won't have to worry about her doing or saying anything to freak her out. That just isn't my mom's style. I'll be shocked if she talks about anything on dry land. Sawyer and my mom are similar that way, able to live without attachments. It sucked growing up that way, but I had my dad to lean on. Shit, my dad.

If anyone was likely to say something to freak Sawyer out, it will be him. I need to remember to text him before we leave. I hope that he'll be cool and not mention anything crazy like getting married or anything. That, sure as shit, would send her running. Dinner isn't for a couple weeks.

I picture her in that yoga pose she was in when I walked in. It was sexy as hell, her strong legs stretching upward with her ass in the air. I carry her toward her room, her lips searching for mine. She can fight me every step of the way, but it's going to hit her at some point, how right we are together.

Her slender arms coil around my neck as I nudge her door open with my foot. Once we're at her bed, I toss her. She lands softly, laughing at me before I launch myself at her. One thing she hates is being treated like glass.

She's tough and stronger than anyone I know. I don't have to hold back. My excitement only turns her on. She's like a powder-keg ready to blow, all nerve endings. I'll never stop wanting to make her lose control, and we have plenty of time.

chapter 8

Sawyer

Dinner was strained at best. I wasn't expecting Jared's dad and his new wife to be there, as well. I guess that after twenty years of divorce, Jared's mom and dad are friends now. Wendy's even staying with them instead of staying at a hotel. Who does that? Vacation at their ex-husband's house? Mr. Keller and his new wife, Jane, are cool, so I guess they don't care; and Jared always said their split was friendly. Wendy's more of a free spirit and tried marriage, but it just wasn't for her.

All through dinner, I feel this expectation to be a couple for them. I don't know how to do that. I avoid Jared's hand when he reaches for mine. When we're seated, I make a point to choose the chair away from his. If they notice anything is off, they don't say so. Jared seems pissed the whole meal, though; that or hurt.

His mom tells us about her new house in Vancouver. She's working for an aquarium up there and studying orca. She seems happy. She hasn't remarried, and as far as I know, she's single. Not every person on the planet is supposed to end up in a couple. His mom's proof of that. I wonder if I'm like her.

Given that she'll only be in town a couple more days, she asks if she can see the progress on the studio before she leaves. I don't even look at Jared before agreeing. We aren't really talking since I freaked out on him. He's even been sleeping in his room again. Now I can't sleep. After dinner, he surprises me by deciding to go back to their house with them, so even though we came together, I'm leaving alone.

It's my own fault. I'm pushing him away, and we both know it. I'm doing it for him, though. He deserves someone who wants all of that. The whole thing, marriage, kids, growing old together; I get hives agreeing to a two-year commitment when I upgrade my phone. The last time I wanted a new phone, I just bought it outright to avoid feeling tied down.

When he never comes home, I feel relief and rejection at the same time. I might be fucking mental. I'm a zombie the next day and am not looking forward to meeting Wendy at the studio. She's waiting by the door when I pull up and park.

"Why didn't you just knock?" I ask, walking up.

"They would have let me in?" She raises a brow at my appearance.

No shower, top knot/pink bird nest on the top of my head, thrift store gem of an old-lady coat, plaid baby-doll dress over jeans, tucked into black combat boots; certain I looked cute, I give myself a quick smell test to make sure I don't reek. The results are inconclusive.

She doesn't plug her nose or breathe through her mouth when she hugs me so I figure I don't stink.

"You look tired."

Ahh, tired. That's what her concerned look is about. "I didn't sleep well. I've scheduled a nap for later." I hold my hand up and add a trigger-finger mouth-click combo before banging on the door.

John opens it, surprised to see me again so soon.

"I have a friend visiting. She wanted to see the place before she heads back to Canada," I explain.

He holds the door open for us and bobs his head in greeting as I introduce Wendy. There are some men assembling cabinetry. They briefly glance in our direction.

"The space is amazing, Sawyer," she gushes once we're in the actual studio.

I glow under her praise. It's a relief. I've always looked up to her. "Thanks, Wendy. It means a lot to me that you like it."

She wraps one arm around my shoulders and hugs me toward her side. "So what's up with you and Jared?"

I sag. "Jared's great. You know that. I'm just not built for long term."

She puts her hands on my back, correcting my posture before ducking her head to look me in the eyes. "Says who?"

"Um, Sawyer says." I laugh awkwardly at my joke.

She sits on a folding chair and gives me her best shrink look. "Why do you feel that way, sweetie?"

"I don't know how to explain it. I just don't do long term, and I haven't ever felt like my world would end if I wasn't with someone," I try to explain.

"I think you're confusing love with obsession. You're already a pro at relationships and an expert at long term. Look how long you've been friends with Jared and Sarah."

"But that's different," I argue.

"Is it? In new relationships, there is always passion, a spark, and an intensity that is all consuming. That doesn't mean that once the newness wears off, there isn't real love there." She stands. Walking over to me, she pulls my hand into hers.

"Don't let your stubbornness stand in the way of your happiness."

"But you're alone, and you seem happy. In fact you seem happier than I've ever seen you."

"I'm seeing someone."

She winks at me when my mouth drops. "Have you told Jared?"

She blushes. "Yes. He gave me the same look you just did. His name is Paulo."

"Shut up." I knock her hip with mine. "What's he like?"

"He works at the aquarium with me, and he's just great."

We walk to a sandwich shop in the same strip mall as my studio, and I pester her until she tells me more about him.

Before we leave, I ask, "You've seemed happy on your own for so long. What changed?"

She takes a sip of her drink. "I don't think I ever made a conscious decision to avoid relationships after the divorce. You know, Jared's dad and I were only nineteen when we got married. Looking back, we were probably too young. With Paulo, it just happened organically."

After hugging her and promising to someday make it up to Vancouver to visit her, I head to Petey's place. We go way back. He's cool, doesn't get all annoyed if I drop off the face of the earth every so often.

I always come back. Last time I saw him was when Will bought Sarah's engagement and wedding rings. I shake my head. Will had wanted to go to the mall. Not for my best friend. I stop by a drive-thru on the way to pick him up a strawberry milkshake.

I flip the sign to closed and lock the door behind me as I call out to him.

"Sawyer, is that you?" He pokes his head around a corner and continues, "How'd it go at your grandma's?"

"All right, I guess. I brought you a shake." I hold the cup up with a grin.

He presses both of his hands to his heart. If he was a preteen girl, he might have also squeed. "Thanks, small fry."

I pass him the shake. "Anytime, Petey. Besides, I need a favor."

His brows touch as his forehead wrinkles. "Whatcha need, kiddo?"

I dig around in my purse until my fingertips brush across the velvet case of my grandmother's ring. "I found this at her house, and," I pause, "I feel like it was important. Can you look at it?"

He motions for me to follow him to his office. He sits behind his desk, and I fall into one of the chairs across from it. I slide the ring across the table to him.

He pulls out a magnifying glass thing and turns on a desk lamp before examining the ring.

"It's a nice setting and a trap cut. Good quality. I'd say it's half a carat."

I nod. "Do you think it's special?"

He moves his glass and turns off the desk lamp. "It's a very nice ring. I have a feeling it was special to your grandmother."

"So, in your opinion, what kind of person would this ring be important to?"

He makes a face and takes a drink of his shake. "I ain't a frufru object whisperer. Why are you asking?"

I pull my knees up and hug them to my chest. "I can't figure that lady out. I guess—I guess I'm scared I might even be like her somehow."

"Like your grandmother?" Petey tilts his head to the side, reading my face like a billboard.

I look at my knees to avoid his eyes.

"Why do you think you might be like her?"

I contemplate avoiding his question. I've known Petey for longer than I've lived in Denver. I figure the whole pulling the Band-Aid off technique is the best way to go. "She didn't love me and didn't want me, and Jared told me he loved me, and I just don't know if I can love him back. Is knowing how to love hereditary?"

I reach out, pluck the ring from his fingertips, and form a fist around it. "Is her holding on to this a sign that maybe she did love stuff, just not me? That's what I want to know."

"Why are you so sure she didn't love you?" he asks gently.

I look back down at my knee. "She didn't want me."

"Said who?"

My head pops up, and I glare at him. "She shipped me off within two days of getting me. I never spent one other night in her house while she lived. If she cared or wanted me, why did she send me to live with other people?"

"Have you ever asked any of the people you stayed with? They clearly must have been close with your grandmother for them to take you in when she asked."

I shrug. I hadn't really thought about it. I groan when I think I was just with Jared's mom, my first caretaker. Why hadn't I asked her?

"You are a genius." I jump up and lean over the desk to kiss the top of his head and grab the velvet case. I tuck the ring back inside before I slip it back into my purse. I flip the sign back to open and take off toward Jared's dad's house.

I'm ringing the bell before I know it.

Wendy's eyes widen when she opens the door. "Sawyer, is everything okay?"

I shake my head. "I just—can we talk?"

She puts her arm around my shoulder and pulls me into the house. "I was about to call for a car to take me to the airport."

"Why isn't Steve taking you? Or Jared? You know you could have asked me over lunch."

She holds her hand up for me to stop. "I had a rental. I stopped to fill it up at the station on the corner, and it didn't restart. I got a lift back to the house from one of Steve's neighbors. He can't leave work. The rental company was going to pick me up."

"Want me to drive you instead?"

"Sure, but you seem upset. Why don't you let me drive?"

I pass her my keys. She calls the rental company and checks out over the phone since the keys to the rental are at the station. If they need anything, they have her number and credit card info already.

She hurries upstairs to grab her bags while I wait for her. I'd offered to help, but she refused.

She passes me her carryon once she's at the bottom of the stairs, and I follow her out to the car. Once everything is in and we're buckled, she tells me to go ahead.

"How well did you know my grandmother?"

"Not that well."

My mouth drops. "How did she know you, to ask you to take me that summer?"

"She knew me through your mom."

I shake my head, trying to understand the confusion evident on my face.

She reaches out to squeeze my hand. "Let me start at the beginning. When I was fifteen, I spent a year in Holland as a foreign exchange student. Your mom's family was my host family."

"So you knew my—"

She nods and finishes my sentence, "Grandparents. I'm so sorry you never had a chance to meet them. Victor and Savina were beautiful people. I will always remember my year with them and your mom fondly."

My mother's father had died of cancer before I was born. Her mother had also been in poor health and followed him less than a year later. Growing up, I remember my mom would tell me my grandmother died of a broken heart.

"Your mom and I became best friends and promised each other we'd go to university together. We picked Dartmouth, only I didn't get in and ended up going to school in Rhode Island."

"But how did my grandmother know to contact you?"

Her look told me to be patient. "I'm your godmother, darling. Your mom and I never lost touch, and after she died, I contacted your grandmother. Agnes was not my biggest fan but was so overwhelmed with grief, I suggested spending the summer with Jared and me would be good for you."

"Overwhelmed with grief?" Disbelief dripped from my tone.

"Of course she was. She had just lost her only son. I don't know what changed over that summer, but her original intention was for you to live with her."

"I don't believe that."

"Believe what you want. It's the truth, though. I'm pretty sure she had even enrolled you in school, too. She asked my advice about back to school shopping."

"Well, clearly something happened because I went straight from being with you to a boarding school in Canada." My tone is harsh.

"Sweetie, I don't know what changed. I only know what was originally discussed. I need you to know that summer with you and Jared was one of my most favorite moments of all time. If I wasn't such a flake, I would have kept you with me all the time, but you were probably better off in Canada, and Jared absolutely was better off here with his dad."

I nod, more confused than ever. If my grandmother had actually wanted me in the beginning, what changed? This conversation leaves me with more questions than I had started with. Wendy pulls up to the curb.

Wendy leans toward me and cups my cheek in her hand. She turns my face to look at her. "Are you okay? Do you want to park? I can call Jared to come pick you up."

I rest my head against her hand for a beat before lifting it. "I'm okay. Just confused and..." I pause. "Confused is the best I got for how I feel."

We unbuckle and hug after she pulls her bags out from the back. "I love you, kiddo. Call me if you ever need to talk about anything."

I bury my face in her hair. "I will. I love you, too."

She pulls back, her hands on my arms. "Be gentle with Jared. Okay?"

"I would never do anything to hurt him. Ever," I blurt.

She pulls me back into her arms. "I know that, honey."

I watch her until the second set of automatic doors close behind her before climbing back into my car. I have to adjust my seat forward before I pull away. I've always been short, but all this thinking about my family these last few days makes me wonder how tall my mom and dad were. They were both taller than I was, in the way all adults were, when they died. If they were still alive, would I be as tall as my mom was or shorter?

My questions swirl on repeat. What happened? What happened? What happened? Why did I go to live with Carmen instead of my grandmother? After I get home, I do a Google search for the school I attended. Carmen had been in her fifties when I lived with her. I'm not sure if she still even works there or is retired. I try calling the school but have to leave a message since it's after business hours.

Frustration makes me antsy. I pace from room to room in a vain attempt to pick up. I've cleared everything off the kitchen countertop and am wiping it down when Jared gets home.

I hear his key in the door and the extra stomp of his boot to knock any snow still clinging to his boots. I hear the clatter of his keys dropping into the glass bowl on the table by the door, the quiet drop of his hat next to it. I'm looking back at the pile of stuff on the island, not feeling like putting any of it back. In my attempt to clean, I've made more of a mess.

"Hey."

I keep my eyes on the pristine countertop in front of me. Maybe I can ignore the mess I've made. If I don't see it, maybe it doesn't exist at all.

He comes to stand beside me, his pinkie finger teasing the edge of my hand without actually taking my hand. He's scoping me out, trying to get inside my head. I drop my head forward, my chin to my chest before rolling it to the side, my ear to my shoulder, my eyes on his.

"I cleaned the counter."

His arm lifts to wrap around my shoulder and pull me closer to him. "That is one clean counter."

He wants me to open up, to tell him what's bothering me. He doesn't want to have to ask.

"I had lunch with your mom today."

"And took her to the airport."

Ah, he knows something. She must have called or texted him after I dropped her off.

"What did she tell you?"

"That you're dealing with some stuff. She didn't say what."

I curl further into him, pressing my cheek to his chest. "She said my grandmother was planning for me to live with her, but something changed."

His one arm stays banded across my shoulders, holding me to him while his other hand strokes slowly up and down my back.

"Isn't that a good thing?" he coaxes gently.

I press my nose into his shirt, nuzzling it as I shake my head.

"Why not?"

I sag against him, knowing he'll hold me up. "I'm just confused now. I wish I knew what changed. Your mom didn't know."

His arms support most of my weight as he walks us to the sofa and sits, pulling me into his lap. "What can I do to make you feel better?"

I offer him my lips in response. His head dips as his lips land on mine. I sink into the solace of his touch. My worries dissolve and flee for now. It scares me how easily I can lose myself in him. The world outside of his skin on mine fades away. The way my body reacts to his feels more than something chemical, more than hormones, and pheromones.

He makes me feel better in a way I've never been able to experience with another person. I straddle him so I can grind against him through his jeans. He pulls my sweater over my head, and instead of doing the same with my tank top, he tugs it down to uncover one of my breasts. He lifts me, bringing my nipple to his mouth. I miss the press of his cock between my legs.

I reach my hand down between us, fumbling with the button of his jeans. I want him inside me. I groan when he gently nips my sensitive peaks.

"Please, Jared, please," I beg.

"What do you want, baby?" he whispers against my skin.

I can't think with his mouth on me. I want him. I don't want to spell it out. I want him to rip off all my clothes, bend me over, and make me forget everything else. I don't want there to be a stitch of clothing between us. I want to feel his skin on mine from the bottom of my feet to the top of my head. I want him to move me. I like feeling light in his arms. I need the delicious burn I'll feel when my body stretches so he can fit inside me.

Knowing he won't move until I say something, I speak, "Give me all you got."

He sets me back down on him. He flips the back cushions off and over the back of the sofa as I pull my tank top off. At the same time that his hands go for my breasts, my hands move to free his cock. He gives my nipples a playful tweak before gripping me by the waist, lifting me and setting me next to him.

He's hanging out of his jeans. He takes off my socks and pants. He leans back for a beat before diving face first into my crotch. My back arches as my fingers find purchase in his hair.

"Oh, fuck," I whisper, locking eyes with him.

My mouth drops as Jared pulls a mouthful of my underwear down my legs with his teeth. I need him to fuck me now. I'm naked, and he still has all his clothes on. Sure, his cock, his rock hard cock, is hanging out, but I want to feel his skin. He tugs his hoodie and the t-shirt he's wearing under it off. I try to move, but he shakes his head and slowly takes off the rest of his clothes.

I'm shaking waiting for him. My hands are too restless to stay still. I roll my nipple between my fingers before pinching it. My other hand drops to tease my wetness. With hooded eyes, he pauses to watch me touch myself. I lick my lips and lift my hips to give him a better view. His desire feeds my own. Just when I'm about to cave and reach for him, he moves to cover me.

My hands move to his neck. I pull his lips down to mine. I sigh into him as he fills me. He waits, letting my body relax around him. My eyes are closed. When they flutter open, his eyes are there to lock onto.

"God, you feel so fucking perfect," he groans, his lips hovering over mine.

My hands slide up to his face, one to each cheek to hold his eyes to mine as he moves in and out of me. My hips meet his with each of his thrusts, but his eyes are what captivate me. I always believed him when he told me he loved me. This beautiful man loves me. I've never felt so scared and alive at the same time.

He sits back on his heels and takes me with him. My hands hold on to his shoulders until he settles himself back down on the couch. My body is now over his. I lean back, arching to feel him deeper inside me. His hands cinch my hips, lifting me and pulling me back onto him. My body takes over. I feel the build within me, the anticipation of release.

"Don't stop, harder. Don't stop," I breathe.

"Get it, babe. Get it," Jared encourages, driving into me.

"Oh, God. Oh…fuck." I ride the pulses out, shaking when they leave me.

They send him over the edge. His hands turn to vice grips on my hips as he spills himself into me. His breaths are ragged as his hands loosen and move to rub the red marks they left on my sides. I lie down on his chest, my ear on one slope as I listen to the thump of his heart. His hands slide up my back and into my hair, rubbing the base of my skull.

I should be sated, blissed out. Instead, I'm overly emotional, raw. Jared's oblivious until a tear slides from my cheek to his chest.

"Hey." He shifts, trying to turn my head to look at me while I turn my face further into his chest. "Are you crying?"

I shake my head, not to say no, but as a silent plea that he not ask. He ignores it, shifting further up so that his back is to the side of the couch and I'm sitting up in front of him. My hands cover my face. I try to hide in the crook of his neck. His fingers wrap around my wrists, and he tugs them from my face. He holds them both in one hand, and he pushes away the hair that has fallen into my eyes.

His thumb brushes my cheek. "Sawyer, why are you upset?" His eyes soften. "Did I hurt you?"

I shake my head.

"Please, talk to me," he urges.

I gulp, swallowing the desire to free any more threatening tears. "You didn't hurt me."

I start to move, but he holds me tight. "I'm not letting you go until you talk to me."

"I just hate that I don't know what happened. I needed her," I admit.

"No matter what, you've got me. " His arms band tightly around me.

Later, as Jared is putting our kitchen back together, he asks me to come to work with him tomorrow.

"Say what?" I can't mask the confusion on my face.

He passes me a take-out menu. Neither of us feels like cooking. "If you stay here, you'll just end up dwelling."

"Well, isn't that what you're technically supposed to do inside a dwelling?" I try to joke.

"You'll feel better if you get out. I'll give you a private lesson."

Something in the way he says it makes my gut drop. I play it off. "You've tried before."

He flashes me a crooked grin, doing his best not to laugh. I can do lots of physical activities. I've been doing yoga so long my balance and flexibility usually make picking up other sports a breeze. Snowboarding is not one of them. Every time I've tried, I've spent most of my time on my ass. Goofy foot or regular, it doesn't matter.

"Come on. I'll make it worth your while."

"Is that so, Keller?"

He grins then nods toward the menu in my hands. "Ready to order?"

chapter 8 ½

Jared

Sawyer watches the tree line out of the side window as I drive. She wanted to drive, but I'm already stressed enough. Besides, my SUV already has clips on the roof rack for my board. I love her, but I'm not letting her drive my ride. I hope this works, getting her out of the condo. She's never been the outdoor sports type, more into yoga than anything else.

I can't wait to get her on the slopes, my turf. She can be as stubborn as she wants anywhere else, but we're heading to my mountain. Once she lets go, she'll see how fun it can be. How right we can be.

Maybe that's the problem. As long as we never leave the condo, she can trick herself into not acknowledging us. Whatever my mom said to her sparked something in her. I don't know what she said, other than encouraging Sawyer to seek out answers from her past. This reminds me of that quote about learning lessons from history or being doomed to repeat it.

When Sawyer and I first started whatever it is we're doing, I mourned the time wasted. We've known each other forever. We could have been together forever. It took me long enough to understand how untrue that is.

I've learned that with every single failed relationship of mine, and watching Sawyer bail on every dude she's been with, how to be the man for her. These years wasted have really been my internship into all the pieces that make up Sawyer Sterling. As much as she likes me to take the lead in the bedroom, she never really gives it all to me.

There's a piece of her that she's still holding back. Maybe getting her outside of her comfort zone and into mine will be the trick. There's also no rush, though. I'd never admit this to anyone but we're light-years farther than I even dreamed was possible. Just because there is no rush, doesn't mean I'm going to stop trying.

Loving Sawyer has made me a greedy man. I can't get enough of her, and I don't think I ever will. She has turned me inside out, and I'll never be the same again. It took me a long time to get this close to her. I've got until the end of time to make her mine. Only thing I can't do is scare her off now that we've come this far.

That would be the biggest mistake of my life.

chapter 9

Sawyer

Getting out is just what I needed.

"You aren't going to push me again, are you?" I tease.

Jared did that once years ago trying to find out which foot was my "dominant" one.

"Nope, you're goofy all the way," he laughs, pushing my knit cap down to cover my eyes.

I push it back up and stick my tongue out at him. After we've parked, he takes my hand and we walk to the snow school together. He hooks me up with a guest pass and gear. I can feel his coworkers checking me out, watching whenever he reaches for my hand. I stand back, surprised when he gives them tasks for the day.

I hadn't realized he was their manager. He stopped competing a couple years ago. He must have gotten more serious about working after that. It's hard not to see him as anything but laid back.

"What?" He drapes his arm around my shoulders as we walk out to the lifts.

"You're like the boss?" I scrunch my face at him, and he laughs.

"What did you think I was doing?"

I shrug. "This is ruining my whole Jared is a bum mindset."

His mouth drops. "Dude, I've never been a bum."

I cover my mouth with my free hand to resist laughing.

He rolls his eyes. "You suck."

My hand still over my mouth, eyes full of mischief, I nod.

It's early and midweek. The resort Jared works at isn't overly busy. As I sit next to him as the lift takes us up, it's clear how at home he is here. Short of when he's drifting off to sleep, I'm not sure I've ever seen him so relaxed.

"Like what you see?"

I elbow him and look at the skiers and boarders making their way down the trail below us. "Thanks for bringing me today."

He slips off his glove, tucking it under his arm, and tilts my chin toward him. His fingers are still warm. He leans down to kiss me. Our eyes lock behind the shaded goggles.

His lips are soft, our kiss sweet. We're nearing the top. He slips his hand back into his glove and takes mine to help me transition off the lift. We are on the bunniest of bunny hills. I've fallen no fewer than six times and I love every minute of it. I'm not thinking about anything other than staying up. There is something so liberating in thinking of nothing else.

If I succeed, I make it down the hill without falling. If I fall, it is within my power and control to try again. Two hours into it, I tag along with Jared as he teaches a beginner group lesson. I am his example. He's off his board, his hands on my hips as he explains to the boarders how to balance, turn, and safely sit if they feel like they're going too fast.

They're glued to him, attention fully under his command. Even I'm under his spell. I've never seen him give a lesson. I've never seen him manage someone. There are people around, but the first time everyone else is out of earshot, I tell him how fucking hot he is like this.

I bite back a laugh when his eyebrows lift. His goggles move with them. He shifts them up onto his head and kisses me in front of everyone. I've never considered sex in the snow before, but if he said the word, I'd probably go for it.

That is until I wipe out. Sitting on the side of a mountain crying because you turned your hips when you only meant to turn your head, which makes you face plant hard, is not fun.

Jared is in front of me. He doesn't even know I've fallen until he turns his head to glance back at me. My wrist hurts. I ate snow, my nose hurts, and I'm crying so hard I don't know if my nose is bleeding or just running. Jared ditches his board and runs up the slope to me. I'm incoherent. My vocabulary is only head nods and shakes at this point.

He unclips my helmet and eases my goggles off. "Can you stand?"

After I nod, his hands move to my board. One of my boots is still fastened. He frees me as I watch. My cries have dissolved into hiccups.

"Does anything hurt?" His face hovers in front of mine.

His gloves are now off, and his hands cup my hand. I nod, lifting my hand. He slowly slides my glove off and inspects my wrist. I wince when he moves it. He keeps his eyes on mine as he lowers his head to brush his lips across my knuckles. He helps me to my feet, and another instructor I remember meeting from before stops next to us.

"Grab our boards. I'm taking Sawyer to the office," Jared instructs over my shoulder.

We take baby steps down the slope. He apologizes the whole way. I want to tell him I'm fine. I am. I just had the wind knocked out of me, and when I fell, it happened so fast that it scared me. I've gotten fairly comfortable falling on my ass. It's falling forward that I wasn't prepared for.

I feel like such a girl. I spend all my time trying to be big, and one face plant on a bunny hill makes me feel small again. I shrug off his grasp by the time the slope levels out. I need to feel like I can stand on my own.

"I'm so sorry," Jared says for the hundredth time.

Once we're inside, I need all of my extra layers off. I ignore his attempts to help even though my wrist hurts. A pile forms next to me. I don't feel like I can breathe normally until it's all gone, and I'm standing in my socks, yoga pants, and a long-sleeved t-shirt. Jared motions for me to sit down. My socks get wet, and I resist the urge to pull them off too.

He doesn't think my wrist is broken, but he's taking me to urgent care just in case. I cradle my hand and watch him as he gets me new socks from the ski shop and slips my regular boots onto my feet. He is so gentle, so sweet. He would have made an amazing father. That last thought is painful so I try to think about anything else.

I refuse to put my arm back through the sleeve of my coat so Jared zips me into it, my injured hand tucked inside. He guides me back to his car, making sure I avoid any ice patches. He unzips me once I'm in the car so I'll be more comfortable. He cranks the heat, and I tease him for not needing to look up the address to urgent care.

Over the years, he and his buddies have been frequent visitors to this location. "Do you have a preferred guest card?" I tease while he parks.

"It's Caleb who was always getting hurt, not me," he replies.

"Good old Caleb." I feel my cheeks redden.

It just feels weird to talk about a guy I messed around with to his friend, who is the guy I'm currently messing around with. It's not even like Caleb and I saw each other that long. We only dated for a short time when Sarah and I first moved to Colorado. Neither of us breaks the silence that is slowly becoming awkward. I shift to open my door, and Jared hurriedly gets out from his side to come help me.

"I feel like an idiot," I admit, letting him lift me down from the truck. "It's probably nothing."

"It's my fault that it happened."

I smirk at him. "I must have missed you pushing me down."

"Boarding was my idea. You wouldn't be hurt if I hadn't taken you."

"Jared, seriously shut up. I fell. It was an accident. It is not your fault."

He doesn't look convinced.

"I mean it."

The waiting room has an electronic check in that Jared fills out for me. After a short wait, I'm called back, and I don't stop him when he comes with. They do the usual triage stuff; check my temperature and my blood pressure, before we are led to a curtained-off room.

I lie down on the bed and use my coat as a blanket. Why are medical offices always so cold? I doze off and blink when I hear the metal clinks of the curtain moving. I glance over at Jared. He's sitting in the chair just off to the side of the bed, nervously fidgeting with his hat. I look up at the doctor when he clears his throat.

"I heard we took a—" He trails off when his eyes meet mine.

Blake friggin' Wilson. What are the odds the only medical professional I've had sex with in this state works here?

Jared looks between us, wondering why the doctor just stopped mid-sentence.

I pinch my eyes shut and use my good hand gesture to Blake. "Jared, this is Blake. He and I went out a few times a couple years back. Blake, this is Jared."

I open my eyes just in time to see Jared narrow his. Fucking awesome.

Wanting to get the show on the road and the hell out of this urgent care as soon as humanly possible, I point to my hurt wrist and explain my fall as quickly as possible. I sneak a couple of side-glances at Jared, who seems content to avoid them.

Blake was a cool guy and still seems to be. With Jared two steps behind, he walks me over to have my wrist x-rayed. Watching Jared stand stiffly next to him as it's happening is surreal. He guides us back to our room before going off to get the actual printouts.

"Jared, say something," I plead the moment he's gone.

His lips form a thin line, and he shakes his head. Right before Blake walks back in the room, Jared leaves, mumbling something about needing to make a phone call.

I restrain myself from pointing out the fact that the miracle of cell phone technology will allow him to do that right from this room. I hardly listen to Blake when he comes back to confirm my wrist is not broken. I do have a sprain, and he fits me with a brace and a prescription for an anti-inflammatory and a painkiller. He gets me started with a shot in the butt.

"Usually, the nurses do this, but I can't miss the chance to see that ass again," he says with a smile as he preps the needle.

I laugh. I can't help it. I also can't blame him. I do have an adorable ass. What sucks is that's the moment Jared decides to walk back into the room.

Blake leaves, making a point to give me one of his business cards with his cell phone number written on the back. He's gone before I even have a chance to tell him I won't be calling him.

Jared's quiet as we walk out. He still opens my door for me but avoids my eyes as he helps fasten my seatbelt. Running into someone who I used to mess around with sucks, but the way Jared's acting is starting to piss me off. He's making me feel guilty, and I haven't done anything wrong.

"You're acting like you're pissed at me," I venture as we're pulling out.

His hands flex on the steering wheel before his eyes meet mine. "I'm not a jealous guy. That just isn't how I act. I felt uncomfortable watching you with that guy, so I left."

"So, seeing me with him made you jealous?"

He nods, his eyes forward.

"Jared, I haven't talked to Blake in forever." I feel defensive.

"I believe you. It still sucked. I could tell he was still into you."

I reach out to put my good hand on his knee, trying to reassure him. "You do know I'm not like that, right?"

I watch the confusion flash across his face. "Not like what?"

"The type of girl who switches guys out like a hot potato," I answer.

He drops one hand to cover mine, squeezing it. "I never thought you were."

"Then why did you get so upset?" I ask.

A whoosh of air leaves him as he relaxes his shoulders back further against his seat. "All I could think of was how bad I wanted to tell him not to get his hopes up. That you were mine."

I've always been too laid back with whomever I was seeing to deal with possessiveness. My usual move would be to hightail it in the opposite direction whenever I noticed it brewing. Jared saying I'm his scares me more than anything ever before has. I like it.

"Are you going to say anything, or have I pushed you away?"

I look out my window. "This is uncharted territory for me. I've crashed with guys before, but never lived with someone I was seeing. Also, I've never been with someone I have as much history with. I'm not sure I'm right for you, though."

"I am."

I have a voicemail from my old school waiting for me once we get home. I knew I wouldn't have time to text or anything so I had left my cell at home for the day. Apparently, Carmen had retired some years back, but they had forwarded my contact information on to her. Now all I can do is wait and see if she gets in contact with me.

My phone is still in my hand when it starts ringing. I look down and see it's Sarah before glancing up at Jared. His guilty expression confirms my suspicion. He must have texted her or something.

I groan and answer, "It's only a sprain. I swear I'm fine."

I spend the next fifteen minutes telling her all about my fall and glaring at Jared for telling her. She has enough on her plate already. She doesn't need to be worrying about me.

After we hang up, I turn to face Jared. "Why did you tell her?"

He shrugs, not looking the least bit sorry. "You know she would have freaked out if she found out about it after the fact."

He has a point. I just wasn't going to tell him that, though. "Then why didn't you say, 'Hey Sawyer, call Sarah?'"

He walks over to try to hug me, but I avoid his arms and walk toward the kitchen.

"You know you would have put it off, and then forgotten about it," he calls out after me.

My face falls; I know he can't see me. When did he get so good at predicting my behavior? Will nothing I do ever surprise him?

The butt shot painkiller is wearing off so I fill a plastic bag with ice and wrap a paper towel around it.

"Dude, I could have gotten that for you," Jared fusses, coming up behind me.

"I'm not an invalid," I huff, taking my icepack to my room and shutting the door behind me.

Once I'm settled on my bed, I kick myself, wishing he would come in and keep me company. My normal reaction to this situation would be a fight or flight type scenario. In the past, I would either be already gone or picking a fight with Jared until he was. This time, I stare at my closed bedroom door wishing he would walk through it. I am so screwed.

When it finally dawns on me that Jared isn't going to chase me, I go back out into the living room. He isn't home. It takes a couple of minutes to sink in after I find his note on the fridge. He's sorry he upset me, and he's going to give me the space I need.

Just my luck, the first time I fight my internal urge to flee, the guy I want flees instead. It's fucking poetic. One handed, I make myself a bowl of cereal, pop some painkillers, and go to bed.

The next morning when I wake, my wrist is throbbing. I pop a pill and wait for it to kick in before taking off my brace so I can shower. Washing my hair and myself one-handedly sucks. Of course, my stupid ass would push away the guy who would do it all for me.

I pull on a pair of leggings and a sweater dress to avoid dealing with zippers and buttons. Even though Jared is already at work, the condo feels extra empty knowing he didn't' sleep here last night. I have to get out of here. I decide to drop by the studio. There's a chance the right floor materials will be delivered today, so that's a good reason as any to stop by.

Once I'm in my car, I immediately pull out my phone. Instead of texting Jared, I'm distracted by a new email from my grandmother's estate attorney. He wants to know what I want to do with her remains. I sure as shit don't want them. She had been cremated, so her ashes can sit in his office until the end of time for all I care.

I ignore it all together and keep reading. It turns out there is an offer on the house, and he still needs my input on donations to the farm. I read over the offer details. It's pretty much asking price with a request that they have a home inspection, which is standard enough.

They are also asking for the closing to be in thirty days barring the home inspection goes well. I say a silent prayer that the home inspection goes all right, given the age of the house. I email the lawyer back to tell him to accept the offer.

I tell him I need more time for the farm matter. It takes me way longer than normal to type that all out with my brace. The silver lining is my fingers stick out just enough that I don't have to type with my other hand. I'm halfway to the studio before I remember I forgot to text Jared.

I say it repeatedly until I get there so I don't forget. Once I park, I send it; hopeful it will produce my intended results. It's only been one night. I don't want Jared to stay away any longer than that.

I pop into the sandwich shop next door and pick up a carton of coffee and a bag of bagels with some cream cheese for the workers. I order an egg sandwich and a tea for myself before I head over. When she notices my hand, the manager walks over with me to help carry everything.

John opens the door after I knock. "What happened to your hand?" he asks, ignoring my tagalong and the food.

"I'll tell you inside. Now help take these bags so this nice woman can go back to work," I plead.

He relieves her of her load while I thank her again for the help. She leaves with a wave. The smell of fresh-baked bagels distracts the men working as they come to see who brought the food. John grabs one for himself and directs me toward another table before the workers descend on the food.

"Do you feed them?" I joke, unwrapping my sandwich.

"They're animals. Now, tell me about your hand."

I give him the rundown, leaving out some of the more embarrassing parts I had told Sarah.

"I sprained my wrist once," he says, holding his left hand out and twisting it before shoving it into his pocket. "I was carrying some drywall scraps and couldn't see the case to a drill on the floor. I tripped over it, dropped all the drywall and fell. Used my hand to break my fall and messed it up. I'm better about keeping a clean worksite these days."

Luckily, it wasn't as though I had a job my sprain would keep me from doing.

While we talk, I check my phone a couple times to see if Jared has texted me back yet. My face must show some disappointment because John asks if I'm expecting to hear from someone. I apologize. I hate people who can't hold a simple conversation without looking at their phones every two seconds, and here I am, doing it myself.

I drop my phone into my purse and promise myself I won't look at it again unless it rings until I get in my car.

"Still expecting the floor delivery today?" I ask.

John grins. "We just got it unloaded in the back before you walked in. Wanna see it?"

"Do turds attract flies?" I grin.

John laughs at my joke, collecting our wrappers and throwing them away before motioning me to follow him. One pack is already open.

"We needed to make sure they sent the right stuff before we accepted the delivery," he explains.

Reaching out with my good hand, I trail my fingers across the smooth wood of the exposed plank. "It's perfect. I can't wait to see it when it's all done."

He hooks his thumbs into the belt loops of his faded jeans. "I'd say you could help us but not with that hand."

I roll my eyes. "Not handy, so I wouldn't have been able to do much more than watch anyway. How long do you think it will take now that it's here?"

"Floors should take three days. We'll need another day or two to finish up the trim."

"That sounds great," I beam.

John asks me to wait before going into the front room to rally the guys back to work. They follow him back two by two and carry packs of wood laminate back toward the front of the studio. Once they're back to work, I hang back and talk with John for a couple more minutes.

As he walks me to the door, I grab his arm. "I almost forgot to ask. Catherine, my facialist, has a table she wants to have delivered. It's going to go in the first of the two spa rooms. Can I give her your number to coordinate that with you?"

He looks down at my hand on his arm. When I pull it away, he nods, "That's fine."

Once I'm back in my car, I check my phone, still nothing from Jared. My impulse is to be annoyed. I haphazardly put myself out there and expect instant gratification. Logic tells me he is probably teaching a class or his phone is in his car or the reception probably blows on the side of a mountain.

These are all valid points. That still doesn't stop me from wishing he had replied. I scroll through my contacts and text Catherine with John's number. I make a mental check and head home. My wrist is sore, but I skip another painkiller in lieu of an ice pack. My plan is to research the farm my grandmother was sending money to so I can answer the attorney.

Pulling up Google, I type Hamilton Farm into the search field. The first link is one directly to the farm's website. Clicking on it, I gasp when the home page comes up. I grew up on this farm. There's a contact number. I grab for my phone with my bum hand and groan when the brace won't allow me to pick it up. I reach across my body with my other hand and take it.

I dial the number and listen to it ring while I try to figure out what to say. A woman answers. She says, "Hello."

"Hi, is this Hamilton Farm?" I ask.

"It is. How can I help you?"

"My name is Sawyer Sterling."

She doesn't let me get any further. "Oh darling, I've missed you."

Um, excuse me? "Ahhhh."

"Sawyer, it's Miss Bess. Do you remember me?"

I rack my brain. I've never been terrific with names and that was a long time ago. "I'm sorry. I don't."

I feel bad for admitting it. I'd probably be able to place her if I saw her. I'm much better with faces. If she's offended I don't remember her, she doesn't let on. I explain that my grandmother has died and that it's now up to me to decide if we'll be continuing the donation.

"You should come out here. There are lots of folks who would love to see your face, darling."

I try to explain that I'm opening a yoga studio, that I'm needed here, that I was just in New Hampshire. I know what I'm doing. I'm trying to convince myself. Ever since I saw the farm on the home screen of that website, I've felt pulled back to it. Miss Bess must remember me well enough to let me continue my one-sided argument in peace.

A couple minutes later, I agree to come out and let her know I'll call her back once my flight is booked. I'm buzzing when I hang up the phone, a weird natural endorphin-produced high.

I'm going back to the farm. Back to the last place I existed before my parents died.

I'm still glowing when Jared walks in. "You're back," I stammer.

"Are you already breaking up with me?" he asks, lifting me up out of my chair.

"Call a guy your boyfriend one time..." I tease.

"By my count, it's three," he murmurs, dropping his lips to mine.

I pull back. "It felt all wrong when you weren't here."

He presses his forehead to mine. "I'm sorry I left like that. I just didn't know what else to do, and I felt like I was just in your way."

I drape my arms over his shoulders. "I think I like you in my way."

chapter 9 ½

Jared

I need to rein the jealousy shit in now. That will not fly with Sawyer. Besides, that's not who I am. Jealousy is a bitch move. If you don't trust the person, how can you say you love them? I should see it as a compliment, instead of acting like a jackass while she's hurt.

Talk about my plan backfiring. I wanted to get her out of her element and onto the slopes with me. I feel like shit every time I see her banged up wrist. At least she won't have to wear that brace that long. I doubt I'll be able to get her on the mountain again, which sucks.

I want to share the things I love most, other than her, with her. She doesn't seem that bothered by it. Maybe that bugs me most of all. I have a girlfriend that I can't really call my girlfriend. I'm acting like a jealous tool. I'm so strung out on her, I don't even know which way is up anymore. If Caleb saw me right now, he'd laugh his ass off.

I had emailed him after Sawyer hurt her wrist. He knows we're seeing each other. His reply didn't pull any punches when he asked how long I've been in love with her, and if I was in love with her when they dated. He isn't mad. He's a good guy and moved on a long time before he moved away.

He just wanted to know, so I told him the truth. Part of me thinks I fell for her the day she walked onto my mom's boat all those years ago. I definitely was into her before they met and hooked up. Risking a change to our friendship kept me from pursuing anything with her. After years of her being content the way we were, I let it go.

It killed me, watching her with him. As much as I like Caleb, their time together was the hardest for me because I knew he was a good guy. It still sucked but was easier somehow when she hooked up with random losers. I could sense their expiration date right off the bat. She came the closest to making a go at a real relationship with Caleb, and that scared the shit out of me.

She even tried to set me up with Sarah all those years ago. As much as I liked Sarah it was always Sawyer for me. I was at one of my lowest points when I met Kristy. As hard as I tried to make it work with her I still failed. I had decided to once and for all just let it go and give up on the idea of finding a Sawyer stand in.

I would still be letting it go and living with her as the fantasy in my head if she hadn't done what she did at Sarah and Will's wedding. Some days I still wake up and wonder if the last few weeks are just a figment of my imagination. Then I look down, see her sleeping in my arms, and know it's real.

Maybe the realness is what's bringing that jealous side out of me. It's just the first time I've logically had to tell myself that and not hulk smash any guy who hits on her. She's going to get hit on. It happens to me too. None of those girls can hold a candle to her, though.

When I told her Kristy and I talked a while back, she didn't even blink an eye. Sawyer isn't the type of girl to chase after a guy. It was a risk leaving the condo. I was sweating bullets that it was a mistake, that she would call my bluff and make me show my cards. I'm all in with her, even if my actions said the opposite by leaving.

When I saw those three words in her text –I miss you- I dropped what I was doing and went to her. I would have been a few hours faster if my phone hadn't died and I had it on me instead of charging it at work. From someone like Sawyer, so scared of attachments, those three words said so much more.

chapter 10

Sawyer

Jared wants to come with me to Tennessee, but there is no way he can get more time off from work. I wish he could come but also know it's better this way, that I should be doing this on my own. He takes me to the airport. Before arriving at security, he gives me a lingering kiss that leaves me wanting more. I make my way to the conveyor belts and turn to blow him a kiss.

His expression makes me want to turn around and get lost in him. He's addictive that way. I keep moving forward, feeling sad and hopeful at the same time. Over the years, the memories of my parents had dulled. I'm hoping the farm will trigger new ones for me to cherish.

After the plane lands, Miss Bess meets me at baggage claim. Her name and voice over the phone did nothing for me, but seeing her in person does the trick. She has put on some weight since the last time

I saw her but otherwise seems unchanged. She always wore her white blonde hair in a tight bun on the top of her head. I remembered thinking she was a ballerina when I was little.

"I remember you," I exclaim.

"Hey, darling," she smiles. "You sure grew up pretty."

I blush, thanking her. Once we have my bags, I follow her to a beat-up tan pickup truck. The farm is an hour from the airport. At first, the silence seems unending, but once we break the ice, it feels natural talking to her. She does her best to catch me up on the ways the farm had changed after I left. There are new faces and some old ones she said I'd remember.

"So, what'd you do to your wrist?"

I huff, lifting it for her to get a better look. "Tried and failed to snowboard."

She laughs, admitting the same thing would probably happen to her.

When I ask her to tell me how the farm works, and what its mission is, she tells me to wait to have that conversation with Bradley.

"Who's Bradley?" I ask.

She laughs, "I think you know him as Beau."

She laughs harder when my mouth drops. "I remember Beau."

He was two years younger than I was and used to follow me all over the farm. It drove me crazy. I think I called him tag-a-long, like the cookie.

"He runs the farm now," Bess adds.

The image of the kid in my memory rebels against the idea that he has, one, grown up, and two, is mature enough to run a farm. What's even weirder is accepting the fact that I'm older than he is. I still don't consider myself an adult.

When we pull off the main road, a gravel-paved drive winds toward the main house. Bess points out stuff along the way. This farm is not a big operation. Total acreage is just shy of fifty. There are four buildings: the main house, two smaller cabin-style houses, and the barn.

I'm getting one of the cabin-style houses all to myself. Bess pulls right up to its front porch and carries my smaller bag while I heft my larger suitcase out from the back of the truck. It's a log-style cabin. The front door opens to a large living and dining room. There's a wood stove front and center with a puffy, yet dated sofa in front of it.

The dining area consists of a rectangular pine table with three mismatched chairs. Past the main room is a small kitchen. There are two doors at the end of it, one leading to a bedroom, the other to a bathroom.

"Doesn't sleep that many people," I remark.

She motions for me to follow her back out to the main room. There are two oversized wardrobes up against one wall. "Both of those actually hold murphy beds. Don't open that one." She points to the one on the right. "Something is wrong with the hinge, and the bed will just fall on you. Hurts like hell," she adds before turning to point toward the ceiling.

There is a ladder leaned up against the wall behind the wood stove. "There is a loft up there that can sleep four more."

"Why isn't anyone living here right now?" I wonder.

"Most of us live in the main house during the winter to save on electricity. No point in heating this place if there's room over there," she explains.

"I can stay in the main house too," I argue, not wanting to be a burden.

She waves me off. "We're full up. Besides, the whole point of this farm is to lend a hand."

"But I could stay in town at a hotel or something," I try.

The look she gives me stops my protests. I throw up my hands in defeat.

"Come on. I want you to meet everyone." She tilts her head toward the door.

I follow her out front. Since the main house is close to my cabin, she leaves the truck where it is and we walk over together. I don't know why I'm nervous. Meeting new people has never scared me. Maybe that's the difference. There will be people here that already know me, people that knew my parents. I want to live up to their memories of my mom and dad.

The main house is colonial-styled, with a wide porch boasting many wooden rocking chairs. My fingers reach out to skim the worn edge of one as we pass. Bess holds the door open for me. I pause on the threshold, glancing back at the rockers. I used to sit on my daddy's knee and count fireflies.

The memory is so vivid, I feel briefly disoriented when it passes. If the weather was warmer, I'm sure those chairs would be full right now. I give a tight smile to Bess as I continue my way into the house. Directly in front of the door are stairs leading to the second floor. On either side of the stairs are a living room and a dining room.

Each room speaks to the number of people living in the house. There are four couches and two side chairs in the living room and the longest table I've ever seen in the dining room.

"Everyone should be back this way." Bess moves past me, turning her head back to talk.

A hallway running alongside the stairs spills into the kitchen. There are children reading at a small round table while two men and three women fuss around the kitchen. A lot of cooks in the kitchen are all I can think. They all look over at us as we enter the room.

Everyone starts talking at once, and I'm overwhelmed by all of the introductions. It's hard to separate one from another, and I don't know whose hand to shake first. I'm also pretty sure I heard a little girl ask why I have pink hair. I smile in her direction while Bess tells everyone to hush.

"Hi," I wave, turning a half circle so I can make eye contact with everyone in the room.

It was something my dad taught me before he died. "Don't look to see if there is mud on their shoes, Sawyer. Look to see if there is honesty in their eyes." I remember asking him what honest eyes looked like, and he said you knew when you first met people if they don't look you dead in the eyes that they're hiding something. Could be something big or small, but it's there in that moment.

My mom was a fan of a firm handshake. She would say, "No wet pasta," and my dad would tease her saying, "it's limp noodle."

They weren't able to teach me every life lesson, but to this day, I look people square in the eyes when I'm meeting them and have a firm handshake.

"Long time, Huck," a deep voice behind me, pulls me back.

I turn to look at him. Only one person ever called me that. "Beau?"

When he nods, I pinch my lips together to keep my mouth from dropping. Farm life clearly agreed with Beau McIntyre. He's not as tall as Jared but still towers over me. Then again, who didn't? He wears a worn in Red Sox baseball hat, his light brown hair peeking out from the sides. He stands tall and his broad shoulders fill the gray Henley he wears.

I start smiling just thinking of all the trouble we used to get into. Seeing my smile must relax him, and he echoes my grin. There they are, his fucking dimples. I move forward, and he pulls me into a long overdue hug. The sweetness of the moment is short-lived once I inhale.

Rearing back, I try to breathe through my mouth. "Oh, my God, you smell awful."

Everyone behind us starts laughing, and Beau has the decency to take a large step back. "On that note," he winks at me, "I'm going to take a quick shower."

I wait until he's turned up the stairs to breathe through my nose again. This is something I had forgotten about living on a farm. Bess introduces everyone to me by name. There are currently three families living in the main house.

Beau's mom and dad live at the other end of the property in the second cabin. That cabin is a one-room without electricity. They use the wood stove to cook and clean and have an outhouse. Beau and Bess are the only ones in the main house who lived here when I did.

"Once Beau is cleaned up, I expect he'll drive over to the cabin and pick up his folks. I know they're excited to see you."

His parents were best friends with mine. They met some time after my parents graduated from college. The farm has been in Beau's family forever.

I sit with the kids at the table and hang out until Beau comes back downstairs. His hair is still wet from his shower and curls a bit at the ends.

He clears his throat when he walks back into the kitchen. "Hey, Huck. Wanna ride with me?"

I excuse myself from our animated conversation of 'what if there was a hidden island of dinosaurs that were going to come and get us'. Seems one of the older kids is reading Jurassic Park. I bite back a smile when I distinctly hear one of the girls ask if she can have pink hair, too. I follow Beau out and stick my tongue out at him as he holds the door open for me.

"You look so grown up," I tease, walking down the steps.

There's only one truck parked out front so I head toward it.

"That's the funny thing about time," he replies.

I nod. "It sure has been a long time."

He starts toward my door, as if he's going to open it for me. I give him a look as he changes direction to head right to his side. I'm buckling my belt as he opens his door.

He stands there for a minute, just looking at me. "How come it took you so long to come back here?"

I gape at him. "What do you mean?"

He climbs in, shutting his door a bit harder than necessary. "This was your home. It shouldn't have taken you seventeen years to come back here."

My mouth settles in a tight line. I straighten my shoulders and look out the windshield.

After taking a couple of deep breaths, I turn my head back to him. "I was just a kid. Don't you think I would have rather stayed here instead of being shipped off to one stranger after another? It's been seventeen years. Unless you've been following me the whole time, you don't have a fucking clue what it's been like for me. We were friends a long time ago. That doesn't mean you can be a judgmental asshole to me now. If this is how this visit is going to be, you can swing by the cabin so I can pick up my shit. I'll just go home."

His mouth drops at some point during my tirade. "You're right. I'm sorry."

I cross my arms over my chest, still feeling slightly defensive despite his apology. "Good. Don't make me kick your ass."

One of his eyebrows lifts up. He must think he can take me. His dimples make a brief appearance before he schools his features and solemnly nods. He slips his belt on before starting the truck. The radio station blares a metal anthem from Metallica.

"Not country?" I joke as he turns the volume down.

He shakes his head. "I thought we were trying to be friendly."

"So, not a fan of country." I make a check mark in the air. "What else should I know about Beau McIntyre?"

He ignores my question at first. "So, you like country music?"

I shrug, only a little annoyed he's turning the questioning around. "I guess I like a little bit of everything. There are some more folk or bluegrass sounding bands that could be considered country that I love."

He scratches the stubble on his chin. "I do like Mumford and Sons."

I fail at holding back a laugh at how embarrassed he seems admitting that. "All right," I pause to catch my breath, "other than being an undercover country fan," he snorts, as I continue, "what have you been up to the last seventeen years?"

The road to his parents' cabin is rough. I hold on to the 'oh shit' bar to keep from being bounced from side to side as he catches me up.

"Dad had a mild heart attack a couple years back."

He pauses as he takes in my wide-eyed expression. "He's okay, or has been okay. We've made a lot of changes around here since it happened. I've taken the operation of the place and he and my mom moved into the far cabin."

"Why didn't they stay in the main house?"

He smirks. "Come on, Huck. You know my dad. Do you think he would relax if he saw work that needed to be done? Delegation never was his thing. This was the only way we could be sure he would take it easy. It was my mom's idea. Apparently, that cabin was always his favorite."

"Is it helping?" I ask.

"He still feels useful out there, we ran into an issue a while back where some local high school kids thought it was abandoned and were getting high in it. Now that it's lived in, we don't have to worry about that anymore. Plus, he can fish in a small pond. They've only been in the cabin for less than a year and his blood pressure's already getting better."

It was clear Beau would do anything for his dad. His admiration for both of his parents was evident with every word he spoke about them.

I envy that so many of my friends had great relationships with their parents. Will lost his dad a couple years back. Their relationship had been just starting to turn around when he died. For Will's sake, I'm glad. The one positive aspect I had to losing my parents when I was ten was I couldn't remember any bad times with them.

They weren't around for me to rebel against during my teen years, not that I ever did rebel. I lived with Carmen during the school term and spent summers with Jared's family until I was eighteen. Carmen didn't care how I dressed or what I did to my hair as long as my grades were okay.

Jared's mom was all about the adventure; I could only get into so much trouble on a boat in the middle of nowhere. After I graduated, I bailed though, on everyone. I needed to stand on my own two feet. All through school, every break, the girls were always so excited to go home to their families. As much as I loved Carmen and Jared's mom I never saw myself as more than a guest.

I took off, headed down to Florida in search of the sun. I confused attention from boys for playing house. I kept it casual though, wanting a family but leaving town whenever things got serious enough to resemble one. Maybe moving around so much is what made my relationships with guys always gravitate toward temporary, like part of me was always ready to leave.

Beau went to college nearby, living at home versus the dorms. His degree is in social work. I almost ask him why his major isn't more agriculturally related when he explains the mission of the farm to me.

The farm is not for profit. They grow enough to provide for those living on it and to stock local food banks. They also barter for other goods or services like work on the trucks or new tires. Everyone knows how to knit, including any men or boys living on the farm. The entire philosophy is about giving back to the community. They receive private donations as well.

"So that's why my grandmother was sending money every year," I mumble, more to myself than him.

"Say what?" he asks as we pull up to the cabin.*

"Part of why I came out here was to figure out why my grandmother was sending money every year. I couldn't remember the name of the farm, but when I saw it in an email from her estate attorney, I looked it up online and I knew."

His hand pauses on the door handle. "She never told you?"

"Told me what?" His question confuses me. "The name of this place? That she kept in touch?" I pause. "Did she keep in touch?"

He nods then tilts his head as if he might change his mind. "Yes and no. She came out here once, probably two years after you left. I don't remember much except that it was a surprise and I couldn't understand why you weren't with her. Other than the donations, as far as I know, we never heard from her again."

My mouth drops. "She came here?"

He hesitates. "It's just weird to me that you didn't know. I was pissed at you when I was a kid." I suck in air through my nose, ready to blow steam out my ears. He sees my expression and continues, "I know it wasn't your fault. Shit, you lost your mom and your dad. I just was angry that I lost my friend. When your grandmother came, I was angry you didn't come as well. I was a kid, a kid who missed his partner in crime."

The air within me cools. "I didn't even live with her. She sent me away to live with people I had never even met before. Trust me. I wish I could have come back here."

"We can ask my parents if they remember anything else about her. It was a long time ago, and I was little."

I nod. "I'd like that."

The cabin is a smaller version of the one I'm staying in. Just looking from the outside, I wonder if it even has a loft. Beau's mom must hear our approach. She opens the door before I've made it up the stairs.

"Hey, darling," she greets, opening her arms.

Just as when I had seen Bess at the airport, I remember Mrs. McIntyre once I see her. When I was little, she loved to brush my hair. Beau was their only child, and she had always wanted a girl. I was such a terror, climbing trees and roughhousing with Beau. My hair usually resembled a bird's nest. I could remember how gentle she had always been brushing out any tangles.

I step into her embrace, exhaling as her arms folded around me. The smell of homemade soap with honey takes me back to my mom. They didn't always make soap, but when they did, they liked to add honey to the mix. Only Mrs. McIntyre and my mom did that. Her hug smells just like the ones my mom used to give me.

"Joe is taking a little nap, but I promised to wake him up once you got here," she explains, tucking her arm through mine and leading me into the cabin.

"Is he feeling okay?" Beau asks, following us.

My eyes trail hers to rest on the figure sleeping in an armchair by the wood stove. "He didn't sleep well last night. We're just going to stay here for dinner tonight."

Beau nods, his forehead creasing with concern.

"He's just tired, honey," Mrs. McIntyre says, dropping my arm to squeeze his before walking over to the armchair.

I glance up at Beau while she gently shakes his dad. "Sawyer is here, sweetie."

The armchair has the footrest up. Once she's sure he is awake, Beau's mom pulls the lever and pushes down on the rest to lower his feet. He rubs his eyes and blinks a few times before looking over at me. He looks nothing like I remember. Time and his health issues have not been kind to the man who was once my father's closest friend.

He makes no move to stand so I walk over to him. "Hello, Mr. McIntyre."

He squints at me and lifts his hand to shake mine. "Call me, Joe." He squints again. "Am I seeing things, or do you have pink hair?"

I laugh, my hand in his. "I have pink hair," I confirm.

His face breaks into a smile, and for the first time, I see the man who sometimes carried me on his shoulders around the farm.

"My eyesight isn't the best, little girl. I wanted to make sure I didn't need to add whatever the opposite of color blindness is to the list."

Beau's mom motions for me to sit in the chair across from her husband. I glance at Beau as I lower myself into my chair. His eyes are locked on Mrs. McIntyre's in some silent exchange.

Wordlessly, he follows her to the other side of the room. They each grab a chair and walk back over to where we're sitting. Beau sits closest to me, his mother on the other side of him. We make a semi-circle around the wood stove.

"It's good to see your face," Beau's dad says as he winks at me.

"It is," Mrs. McIntyre agrees. "You are the image of your mother."

"Thank you," I smile.

They want to hear about my life after the farm. As I fill them in, I can tell they're just as surprised as Beau had been that I had not lived with my grandmother. I try to sell how happy I am, how many good friends I have, and what I did to my wrist.

"Any boyfriends?" Mrs. McIntyre asks, glancing at Beau.

I hesitate. "I am seeing someone. I've never been that into labels, Mrs. McIntyre."

"Sawyer, call me Lynn, please." She puts her hands on her hips. "So tell us about this young man. Is it serious?"

I don't even know I'm smiling until after Lynn remarks that my face lights up talking about him. "It did?" I ask.

She nods then looks back at Beau. "If only Beau could meet someone. He's not getting any younger, and someday—"

"All right, Mom. I know, I know." He looks at me. "My mother likes to remind me it's tradition to pass the farm on to the next of kin, and I'm currently lacking."

Hearing him talk about family just reminds me that if I never have kids that's it for both sides of my parents' families. It would all end with me. It reminds me that I also don't know why my grandmother visited the farm.

Clearing my throat, I ask, "What made my grandmother come here?"

Joe's eyes flick to Lynn before he replies, "I guess she was curious. I don't think she fully understood what your parents were doing living here."

"She thought we were a cult," Lynn adds.

"Excuse me?" I gasp.

Joe nods. "Your grandmother, Agnes, was a piece of work. I guess somewhere in your dad's will, he asked that some money go to help keep the farm going. My best guess is she wanted to make sure we weren't up to no good before any money came to us."

"She also seemed to think we'd come after you when I told her how much we missed you. It took her some time to change whatever opinion she had of this place," Lynn murmurs.

I shake my head. "Seriously? A cult?"

Joe shrugs. "Cult may be a strong word. From the outside, we seem like a bunch of hippies, and looking back, we kind of were."

Lynn laughs at my expression. "We wanted to live simple lives, live off the land, help those around us. To a certain extent, it's still that way."

I tilt my head. "Like how?"

She leans back into her chair, resting her hand on Joe's arm. "Have you seen any TVs since you've been here? Any iPods, or pads, or whatever those game things are called?"

I glance around, feeling silly once I remember this cabin has no electricity. I think back to my cabin and the living room of the main house. I don't remember seeing any electronics. I also didn't have to talk over a device when I sat with the kids in the kitchen.

"But you have a website," I look at Beau.

He nods. "We do need a website for a virtual link in the community. We also have radios to keep us posted if there are any storms. Depending on how they're doing in school, sometimes the kids get to watch a DVD on my computer."

"What do their classmates think? Do they have any issues at school?" I ask, curious.

"They're all homeschooled," Beau replies.

I gape. "Don't they get bored?"

He shakes his head. "There are tons of kids that are homeschooled nowadays. Besides, there's plenty to do and learn on the farm."

"How do they keep up with their grade level? Can they go to college?"

Beau grins at my questions. "You're looking at one kid who did."

"You were homeschooled while you lived here too, Sawyer," Lynn adds.

My forehead wrinkles. "I was?"

She nods. "What did you think you were doing?"

I shake my head. "I just remember being free-range and playing in the orchard."

She smiles. "The secret to the best learning is when you don't know it's happening."

Jared

This condo is so empty without her. For someone so small, she really fills up the place. I miss her. I knew I was going to, but I don't understand the full impact of just how much until I have to fall asleep without her. I'm sitting here, on the sofa, eating a bowl of cereal. Each bite I take and chew sounds louder than possible.

I flip on the TV so there is some illusion that I am not alone. I wish she'd let me come with her. Will distance be all it takes for her to have second thoughts about what we're doing? It'll kill me to lose her.

Just sitting here doing nothing is fucking with my head.

I've been thinking about doing something ever since we went through her grandmother's house. It could backfire big time, but it's better than doing nothing at all. I carry my unfinished breakfast to the kitchen and dump it in the sink.

Then I grab my cell phone and call the East Coast. It takes four calls to set my plan in motion. As I head to take a shower to get ready for work, I feel more energized than I have since she left. Now I feel like I have an ace in my back pocket. I just can't wait for her to come home so I can play it.

I have a class of beginners first thing today. We keep them in a fenced off area for most of the lesson. There are six kids total. One requirement is that they wear helmets. It only makes sense, and it's fun to knock on them when they aren't paying attention.

It's the lessons with the littlest kids that always remind me how close I was to being a dad. Sawyer would run so fast and so far if she had any idea that I've pictured her having my baby. From what little we've talked about kids, I'm pretty sure she doesn't see them in her future.

I'm cool with that, but I don't think she saw me in her future either. Maybe, once I know she isn't going to bail, I can ask her if she'd even think about it. If it isn't something she wants, I'll just have to play Uncle Jared to someone else's kid. I would be a badass uncle.

I glance down at the kid who just face-planted in front of me.

"Dude, you okay?" I ask, helping him up.

His toothy grin is infectious, and I laugh as he hurries to board down again.

chapter 11

Sawyer

Joe seems tired by my visit so Beau and I leave not long after that with Lynn's promise to come visit me at my cabin. I still have so many questions for her. Beau and I are quiet as we drive back to the main house.

Before getting out, I turn to him. "I'm sorry about your dad."

He fiddles with the keys, looking straight ahead. "It's hard to see him like that. It just seems like he's winding down."

"Don't say that. Now that he can rest, maybe his health will improve." I try to comfort him.

"That's the goal. I'm lucky for the time that I have with him. I can't imagine what you went through."

"You can't?" I ask. "They acted like a second set of parents to you. I remember thinking of your parents that way."

"Your leaving hit me harder. I would wake up every morning thinking it had just been a bad dream and that you would come back."

"Those days were so confusing for me. I didn't even know what to think, but I was lucky I had Jared to lean on. Who became your Huck?"

"No replacing you, Huck. Time and getting more responsibilities around the farm are what did it. Come on. We should head inside. It's about time for dinner."

I follow him into the house, my heart breaking for the boy who lost his best friend when I left the farm. He seems no worse for the wear, so I do my best not to dwell on that thought. Besides, the smells coming from the kitchen cannot be ignored. I glance into the dining room and see the table has already been set.

I trail behind Beau into the kitchen. "Can I help out with anything?"

Bess waves me over. "Wash your hands, and you can help slice the bread for dinner."

After I carefully wash my hands, avoiding my wrist guard, she sets me up with a warm loaf of freshly baked bread. My stomach grumbles as I slice it. We all move to the dining room not long after. Beau hollers up the stairs for a couple of kids to come down.

Once everyone is seated, Beau turns to me and raises his glass. "To old friends."

"To old friends," everyone repeats clinking glasses.

The meal is a simple one: pot roast. Large chunks of roast mixed with potatoes, carrots, celery and a beef broth. The fresh bread is perfect for dipping in the sauce. While I lived with Will's mom, I convinced her I was a vegetarian. I don't eat a ton of meat at home. I basically live off of processed foods. It's clear this meal was made from scratch, though.

"This is delicious," I sigh.

"Comfort food," Bess smiles at me from across the table.

"I feel extremely comforted," I joke.

After dinner, I jump up to help Beau clear the plates.

"I'm on dish duty tonight," he explains as I follow him to the kitchen.

"I'm a pro at dishes. You wash, I dry?" I offer.

"Works for me, but dishes can wait until after dessert," he says, setting his stack in the sink.

Two of the kids from earlier hurry around us to collect the dessert and dishes for it.

"What are we having?" I ask as I try to see what one kid is carrying.

He grins and lifts a mouthwatering chocolate cake.

"Is that my piece?" I tease, "What are the rest of you going to eat?"

He laughs. "No, silly. This is for all of us."

I pout. "Well, I suppose I can share this one time."

Beau comes up behind me. "Note to self: Sawyer is still a fan of chocolate cake."

I nod, and we follow the cake bearer back to the dining room. Conversation is light over dessert. Once Beau mentions to the group that I've done some traveling, that's all they want to hear about. Seeing the younger ones' expressions as I describe some of the places I've been is too much fun.

"You've actually ridden on an elephant?" The cake bearer, whose name turns out to be Trevor, is suspicious.

"I have. I spent a month staying at an ashram in India." I try to keep my expression serious so he won't think I'm teasing him again.

It hits me then that, minus the meditation, this farm is not unlike the ashram where I stayed. It had a community feel where we would all pitch in to make sure the chores that needed to be done were done. No matter who we were or where we came from, we all worked together.

After dessert, Beau and I head back to the kitchen to tackle the dishes.

As he hands me a plate to dry, he pauses. "I'd like to take you someplace tomorrow if that's okay."

I hesitate. "What time do you think your mom will stop by?"

He reaches out for the next plate. "Probably early, we can go after you're done talking with her."

"That sounds good. Where're you taking me?"

He leans his hip on the counter and shakes his head. "You'll just have to wait and see."

"No fair," I grumble, flicking my index finger in his direction.

He dabs his cheek with the dishtowel. "Now, I'm really not going to tell you." He empties the sink and refills it when we get to the pots and pans.

"Might need to let these soak overnight," I say, peering into the pan that the roast was cooked in.

Beau argues with a laugh, "You just need to put a little muscle behind it."

I watch as he works on the pan. He definitely has me beat in the muscle department.

"Other than dishes, anything I can help out with around the farm while I'm here?" I ask as he passes the now clean pan to me.

"I'm sure we can find a way to keep you busy," he jokes before flicking suds at me.

I manage to get the towel up in time so the water hits it and not my face. Peeking out from behind it, I stick my tongue out at him before lowering it.

"I still don't get her," I confess.

"Get who?" Beau asks, turning off the water.

"My grandmother. She visits this place, but she never attempts to see me. Who does that?"

He eyes me cautiously. "Do you wish you would have reached out to her before she died to talk about this?"

I shrug, setting the plate down and turn to lean against the counter. "This might sound awful, but I never thought about her. I missed my parents, but I spent such a short amount of time with her. Maybe I'm only curious now because she's gone. Does that make me a bad person?"

He pulls the towel from my hands and loops it over the handle of the stove. "Bad for what? Not staying in touch with her? As far as I'm concerned, the lines of communication go both ways. You were so young when your parents died; I think she should have made the effort then to stay in your life."

"I get what you're saying. I do. I just feel like maybe I wouldn't have so many questions now if I would have tried to have a relationship with her."

"Coulda, shoulda, woulda, Sawyer. Time for second guessing yourself is over."

I move toward him, wrapping my arms around his waist and tucking my head under his chin. His arms hesitate before banding around me tightly. Beau is the closest thing I ever had to a brother. He holds me until Miss Bess pops her head into the kitchen to ask if we need any help.

Beau drops his arms and replies, "Nope, just about done."

After everything is clean and dried, I follow him out to the front room where the adults are gathered. The kids are across the hall playing Uno on the dining room table.

"They'll be going to bed soon," Beau nods in their direction.

"It's so early," I argue, my body disagreeing as I stifle a yawn.

"Are you tired, Sawyer?" Bess asks, watching me.

"A bit," I admit.

"I'll walk you over to your cabin," Beau says, taking my hand.

He follows me in briefly to make sure I'm settled and to double-check if I need anything. Once I assure him I'm fine and he leaves, I call Jared.

I smile when he answers on the first ring. "Sawyer?"

"Who else?" I tease.

There's a pause. "How are you?"

I've never been good at lying. "I miss you."

"I can fly out tomorrow if you say the word."

I still can't lie even though I wish right now that I could. "I need to do this on my own."

He huffs, "Why? I get that you're independent and can take care of yourself. I'm not trying to change that. I only want to be there for you."

"I know. I just…" My voice trails off.

"It's okay, but if you change your mind, I'll be on the first flight."

I tell him the little bit I learned of my grandmother and that Beau's mom is coming to see me tomorrow to talk some more. He asks about Beau. I wonder if he is worrying that I'll seek comfort in him because he's here. I can't think of a way to ease his potential concern without implying something that may not even exist.

We linger on the phone, long after all conversation ends. After exhaustion finally prompts me to say goodbye, I fall asleep stubbornly hugging the phone. I wish I were in Jared's arms instead.

When I wake to find it still pressed to my chest, I groan at my own lameness. I'm stronger than this. Deciding a shower will clear my mind, I head straight to the bathroom. The plumbing is dated. I start to wonder at my own intelligence until I finally figure out how to get the shower going with hot water.

I don't bother drying my hair, twisting it up into a loose pink bun that doesn't match the pale blonde growth of the rest of my hair but still works somehow. My wrist doesn't feel as sore today, so I decide to skip my guard for the day. Since it isn't broken, I don't need to wear it that long. Besides, I can always put it back on later.

I can only assume everyone at the main house has finished breakfast before I even woke up. I rummage through the small kitchen and am pleasantly surprised to find it stocked with your standard fare. I scramble an egg and make some toast. I brought tea with me so I boil some water in a small pot. I've just finished and am cleaning when Lynn knocks.

"Good morning," I smile, holding the door for her.

She kisses my cheek as she passes in front of me. I follow her to the timeworn loveseat in front of the wood stove. Tucking my feet under me, I wait for her to speak first.

"I loved your mother like she was my sister. When your parents moved to the farm, we were inseparable."

I try to picture them together, maybe slowly walking after Beau and me as we tear off into the orchard.

"Your parents loved you very much."

I give her a tight smile. "I know."

She reaches over to squeeze my hand. "Of course you do. This farm will always be your home. I hope you know how much we all still love you, darling."

Always be my home.

Hearing those words is like she just smoothed a Band-Aid across the skinned knee that is my fragile heart. "But my grandmother…"

She senses the uncertainty in my statement. "Agnes Sterling was something else. I don't know why she sent you away, but I do know, after she was certain we weren't after you for some nefarious purpose, she relaxed. That has to say something."

"Did she know I was happy here?" I ask.

"I hope so. She wasn't the most forthcoming."

"But if she knew that, why didn't she just let me come back here?" I argue.

"I can only theorize, Sawyer, because only she truly knows the answer to that question, but I know she wasn't pleased with your father's decision to move here."

"I get that she could feel that way before she understood the work you do, but why after?"

"It was maybe six months after you left that she came to visit. Is it possible she didn't want to disrupt you further? That you were settling into your new home."

I shrug, not wanting to lie but not able to agree with the logic in her words verbally either. "What was she like?"

She pauses, thinking about it. "The only way I can think of to describe her is as a force of nature. Taking no for an option was not a possibility for her. Once she was satisfied we weren't up to no good, she tried to take over."

"What?" I ask, confused.

"Not really, but it felt like it at the time. That woman had opinions for everything and had no problem giving them to us whether we asked for them or not."

"Did she know stuff about farming?"

Lynn laughs. "Not as much as she thought she did."

"Why do you think she didn't keep me?"

Lynn's face falls. "I don't know, sweetie."

After she leaves, I almost call Jared, but it's still early and I don't want to wake him. I'm lost in my thoughts when I hear a knock on the door. Glancing at the clock, I realize I've missed lunch. I pad toward the door, trying to ignore the grumble of my annoyed stomach.

"Hey, Beau."

He takes one look at me. "You okay?"

"I forgot to eat lunch. Do I have time to inhale something?"

"Sit," he gently commands. "I'll make you something."

I start to argue, but he cuts me off. So, I plod over to the loveseat, slump into it, and watch him. In no time, he carries over a plate with a peanut butter and jelly sandwich on it.

"Thank you," I say, before taking a bite.

He shrugs as if it's no big deal. In that moment, unexpected anger pools within me as I mourn the relationship Beau and I never had. I coveted the bond my best friend Sarah had with her brother, Brian. Something tells me if I had never left, that could have been Beau and me.

He fills the silence by telling me what he did over the morning while I visited with his mom. There's pride in his tone as he tells me about fixing an old tractor. After I finish my food and set the plate in the sink to wash later, we leave.

"Any hints as to where we're going?" I joke.

His face is solemn. "It's a special place."

We drive in the direction of his parents' cabin but turn off onto another worn dirt road before we reach it. We're headed toward the far edge of the orchard. It's familiar, dawning on me before I can see the simple headstones.

I reach out for the door handle, already squeezing it even though we haven't stopped.

"Are they…?" I ask, staring out the window.

I hear his gulp. When the truck stops, I tumble out and rush over to the small grouping of graves. Tears cloud my eyes, but they don't stop me from finding them. Their stone rests near the apple trees.

The limbs are bare now, but knowing they shade my parents feels right. I sink to my knees in front of their shared headstone and let my tears fall freely.

Beau kneels next to me and puts his arm around my shoulders.

> Henry & Abigail Sterling
>
> "Age saw two quiet children
> Go loving by twilight-"
>
> Loving parents and the truest
> of friends.
> Gone too soon from this
> world.
>
> Rest in Peace.

"I never even thought to ask where they were buried. Was there even a funeral? Why wasn't I at my own parents' funeral?"

He looks away. "The headstone is more of a place to come mourn them. Funds were tight. It took a couple years for my folks to get it. I don't think there were any remains."

"Remains." I gulp down the bile crawling up my throat. "Of course."

"Shit. I'm sorry, Huck."

"Can I have a minute?"

He shifts to his feet and walks away.

My index finger traces their etched names on the cold stone. "Hi, Mom, Dad."

Words like tears pour from me. I tell them how much I miss them, how much I'll always miss them. How I hope that, no matter what, they would be proud of the person I am today. I tell them about Jared, Sarah, and my yoga studio. I don't stop talking even though my throat starts to hurt and cold seeps from the ground through my knees, making my whole body shake.

After I run out of stories to tell them, Beau comes back to sit with me. He gently tugs me to his side, and we sit together a while longer.

"The quote?" I ask.

"I think it's Robert Frost. My dad would know for sure."

"I found a book of his poems in my dad's old room," I pause, looking forward again. "Thank you for bringing me here."

Beau drops me back off at the cabin afterward. I need to be by myself, and he seems, instinctively, to know. I climb the ladder and sit on the bed in the loft. There's a port-style circular window overlooking this side of the orchard. My parents' stone is on the other side. There are too many trees even to hope to see the small cemetery, but

216

somehow it gives me comfort just knowing it's there.

I wonder if they ever took my grandmother there, and what her reaction was to it if they did. If Lynn is at dinner tonight, I'll ask her, or maybe Bess knows. I came here to try to learn more about my past, but somehow I'm being left with even more unanswered questions than what I started with.

The buzz of my cell sends me clamoring down the ladder for it.

I glance at the screen before answering. "Jared?"

His voice cloaks me in warmth to where I can almost feel his arms around me.

"How are you?" I ask, not wanting him to stop talking.

He misses me but wants to give me the space I need. Carmen's cousin called the house phone. He's calling to give me her number and tell me what her message said. Apparently, Carmen is in poor health, now living with her in Arizona.

Before we hang up, he says, "Know nothing has changed for me."

He still loves me.

I can't say the words back. I don't know how.

"Jared," I start.

"We'll talk later." And he's gone.

Jared

I rush to hang up with her. There is shit she needs to deal with and me begging her to come home will do nothing but interfere with that. The ache of her absence still throbs within my gut every day, but I can't hold her back.

She needs to find out why her grandmother did what she did. I only hope that once she knows, it won't haunt her anymore. As much as I miss her, I understand now why she needs to do this. As crazy as my mom is, I've always known she loves me. My dad balances her crazy by being this rock I can always lean on.

Sawyer has Sarah and me. I know we are no less there for her than my parents are for me, but I get that it's different. She went years not feeling that. From what Carmen's sister said in the message, I hope Sawyer gets there in time to talk to her.

The worst-case scenario is if she isn't able to find out what happened. I feel shitty for ending the call like I did, though. I pull on my coat and head to the door. I'll swing by the studio and check in with John. He's a good guy. I'll text some pictures to Sawyer and let her know I'm thinking of her.

John is locking up when I pull up.

"Hey, John," I call out, hopping out of Sawyer's Hummer.

I took it so I could fill it up for her before she gets home. When she gets home.

"Jared." John holds out his hand, grinning.

"I'm glad I caught you. Would it be cool if I took some pictures to send to Sawyer? She has a lot going on. I think they'd cheer her up."

"Sure, man." He turns and unlocks the door. "I'll show you what we finished up today."

After warning me where paint is drying, he shows me around the studio. The floors, walls, and cabinets are done.

"Dude, this looks great," I say, pulling out my phone.

"We need to do a bit more in the bathrooms but should be done soon. Do you know when Sawyer will be back?"

I shake my head. "She should be on her way to Arizona. A family friend is ill."

"That's too bad. She'd be thrilled to see all the progress we've made. We even managed to get that giant table of Catherine's in."

"I can let her know next time we talk. It was a table? Like a massage table?"

"Yep, want to see it? It weighed a ton."

Somehow I assumed getting a facial would be like getting a hair cut, in a chair. "I didn't know they do the facials lying down.

"Facials?"

I shrug. "Cleans out pores, I guess."

We share a look. Women.

chapter 12

Sawyer

After talking to Marie, Carmen's cousin, it's clear I need to leave right away. I let her know I'll book the next flight and call her once I land. Beau is standing in front of the door when I open it. It's almost dinnertime.

"Can I use your computer?"

"Everything okay?"

I explain on the way over, and he takes me right up to his upstairs office. I book the first flight to Tucson I can find and quickly say goodbye to everyone before Lynn and Beau take me back to the cabin to pack.

"I'm so sorry about this," I say, cramming clothes into my suitcase.

"Don't worry your pretty little head, darling. This won't be the last time we're together. I'm sure of it."

On the way to the airport, she confirms my suspicion. When my grandmother visited, they took her to visit my parents' headstone. She knew it existed and never told me. Hate is an emotion I normally only reserve for people who prey on those weaker than themselves.

How can I hate my own grandmother?

There isn't time to linger once we reach the airport. I give a quick hug and kiss to both Lynn and Beau, and I make my way to security. Once my suitcase is on the belt, I glance back at them to wave one last time. Beau's arm is around his mom's shoulders.

It strikes me at that moment our roles could easily have been reversed. His father had also been a small craft pilot. It could have been his parents. Beau could have lost his parents instead of me losing mine. What ifs are dangerous to accepting the life that you have. History was not meant to be rewritten. I can only live in my present.

When I reach my gate, I call Jared to let him know. He doesn't ask if he should get a flight and meet me there. It doesn't bother me, though, because I know he would come if I asked. He updates me on the studio progress. Our doors will be ready to open in less than a week whether I'm there or not. I end the call when my plane starts boarding.

As we prep for takeoff, I think of all of the ways Jared takes care of me. I'm used to being the one who takes care of everyone else. It's what I do well. I'm a problem solver. I'm independent. People need me more than I need them. I don't need anyone. I don't.

When we land, I rent a car. It has GPS, and it saves Marie from having to get someone to come get me. Also, the forty-five minute drive will give me a chance to charge my cell. I plug my nearly dead phone into its car charger and call Marie and text Jared before I leave.

I'm making great time until I see the flashing red and blue lights in my rearview mirror. Shit, how fast was I going? Couldn't have been that fast. I pull over onto the shoulder and kill the engine.

The police officer looks like Seth Rogen. I suck my lips to avoid laughing when I think about the movie *Super Bad*. Different kind of cop, different kind of cop, I repeat to myself internally.

"Do you know why I pulled you over?" he asks after asking to see my license and registration.

I shake my head.

"I clocked you going sixty-nine in a fifty-five."

Sixty-nine? Don't laugh. Don't laugh.

"That's almost reckless speeding."

Shit. That sobers me up. I do not need another one of those on my license.

I've also learned over the years that police officers don't want to hear your sob stories. Unless you are in labor or some other similar type emergency, they don't care.

I sit quietly while he writes my ticket. I wait for him to pull out first then go. It would suck to be pulled over twice in the same day, so I use cruise control the rest of the way.

Marie lives in a small retirement community. I pass condos and a hospital-like retirement home before finding her street. She lives in a house. It's a small, adobe-style ranch.

It's late. I start to feel guilty for showing up at this hour, but I don't want to miss an opportunity to talk with Carmen again. There's a light on in the front room, and I see the curtain move as I pull my suitcase up the front walkway.

A woman, who I can only assume is Marie, opens the door before I have a chance to knock.

"Hello, Sawyer."

She could be Carmen's twin. The family resemblance takes me back to my school days in Canada.

"Hello, Marie. Thank you so much for letting me stay with you."

"Is nothing. Come, come."

She reaches for my suitcase, and I follow her into the house after quietly closing the door behind me.

She points to Carmen's room and holds her finger to her lips to let me know she is sleeping before showing me my room.

The time difference zaps any energy I have. I don't even bother changing before collapsing into bed.

I wake to hushed voices the next morning. After popping into the bathroom to freshen up, I go find them. They're both in the room Marie gestured to the night before. Carmen is sitting up in a hospital-style bed as Marie sits in a chair next to her and feeds her what looks like oatmeal.

Where Marie looks like the Carmen of my memories, Carmen herself looks so different. Her once raven hair is now full white. She never left her room without her hair done and her fire engine red lipstick. Now her skin's pale, her lips dry. She used to have beautiful hands, and I would keep her company while she painted her nails. They're now gnarled, her knuckles sticking up like cracked roots around an ancient tree.

"How is she?" I ask Marie.

"I am not *sorda*."

She is not deaf. I meet Carmen's eyes and feel ashamed for losing touch with her over the years. I spent most of my summers with Jared and his mom, but during the school term, Carmen raised me.

"How are you?" I hold her gaze and walk closer to her bed.

Marie moves from her chair so I can sit and offers me the bowl so I can help Carmen eat.

When she reaches for me, I set the bowl down and clasp her hands.

"*La mia Sawyer*."

Her Sawyer. "*La mia Carmen*."

Her eyes crinkle as we just look at each other. I have questions for her, but I don't want to overwhelm or tire her with them. Time has shrunk the woman who once was larger than life to me. She had always seemed like a force of nature, an unstoppable force. She was what I always wanted to be when I grew up.

When I was still in school and I would tell her this, she always reminded me never to grow up, that that was the trick of it all. I've kept those words with me all these years.

She drifts while I sit with her, and Marie beckons me to follow her to the kitchen. There she makes me tea and offers me breakfast.

"How is she, really?" I ask.

She drags a pack of cigarettes across the counter, taps the pack a couple times then pulls one from it. After lighting it and taking a long pull, she breathes out a cloud of smoke.

"She sleeps more each day and does not eat. Is no good."

I shake my head. "Is there anything I can do?"

She shrugs. "She is happy you are come. That is good."

Because I am here, Marie uses the opportunity to run to the store and pick up some groceries. She is looking forward to having someone to cook for tonight.

After I shower, I go back to sit with Carmen. "Carmen, there was a ring I found in my grandmother's house. It was simple…"

She lifts her hand, cutting me off. "It was her wedding ring."

"What ever happened to my grandfather?"

She shakes her head. "One day he just left. She wore the ring for years, hoping he would come back. When she took it off, she said she would never love again."

"Never again?"

Carmen nods slightly, her eyelids heavy.

I start to stand. "I should let you rest."

She lifts her hand again to stop me and points to a book next to her bed. The woman who read me stories at night wants me to read to her. Life truly does have a way of coming full circle.

It's an Italian translation of Little Women. The book is so worn I wonder if it's the very one she read to me when I was little. I don't ask. I just read. By the time Marie is back from the store, Carmen is asleep again. I help her bring bags in from her car and then unload once they are all in the kitchen.

We talk more about Carmen's condition. She is diabetic and her kidneys are failing. She isn't healthy enough to be considered for a transplant. At this point, her body is just shutting down. A hospice nurse stops by weekly and more frequently if Marie calls her.

Keeping Carmen as comfortable as possible is their focus.

Once everything is put away, she squeezes my arm. "You should try and talk to her."

I nod and head back to her room. She's asleep, but I sit in the chair next to her and wait for her to wake. When she does, my presence seems to startle her. Marie hurries in to explain again, who I am. Could she have forgotten me? My heart tightens as I watch for a sign of her knowing me.

"Sawyer. Sawyer," she rasps.

I reach my hands out to hers and let her fold them into her grasp once she is calm.

"Talk now," Marie orders.

I take a deep breath. "Carmen." Deep brown eyes fixate on mine. "Why didn't my grandmother want me to live with her?"

She shakes her head.

I lean forward. "Why did she send me to you?"

"Agnes had problems."

"What kind of problems?"

"Marie."

"Marie knew my grandmother?" I ask, confused.

She shakes her head.

"Do you want Marie?" I glance out the door.

When she nods, I stand and go to get her. "She's asking for you."

I follow her back to the room and watch as she leans close to Carmen, listening to her. Whatever Carmen says is too quiet for me to hear.

Marie stands and comes to me. "There are some things she has for you that may answer your questions."

She turns and walks to the closet and pulls a box out from under some blankets. It's the size of a shoebox.

"She wants you to have this."

"Should I sit with her more?" I ask, looking over at Carmen.

"Yes." She nods. "Then you help me cook."

I can't suppress my smile, and I lean over to kiss her cheek. She pats my back and winks at me before heading back to the kitchen. I tuck the shoebox under the chair and start to read to Carmen again.

Marie comes back with soup for Carmen and tells me to take a shower because we will have company for dinner. I take the box with me and leave it on my bed. After my shower, I change into black jeans and a blue sweater. It's the dressiest thing I have with me. Carmen is sleeping, and I find Marie in the kitchen dicing tomatoes.

It's nice to relax and just follow Marie's directions. We're making an old family chicken recipe and a friend of the male persuasion is coming over for Marie. Once everything is prepped and cooking, she goes to her room to get ready.

"You look smokin' hot," I gush when she comes back out in a low cut dress that hugs her curves.

She flounces her hair and gives me a sexy pout.

"Why didn't Carmen ever get married?" I ask, remembering how sought after she had been while I was in school.

She lights a cigarette. "She never want to settle down. I think if she had it to do again, she perhaps act differently."

"Was there anyone in particular?" I ask, trying to remember.

"I know there was a man. She loved him very much, but she was a proud woman. She would not change."

"I know a bit about that," I admit, thinking of Jared.

"There is a man you love?" she asks.

"He loves me. I love him, but I don't know if I love him, love him."

"What is this love him, love him?" She waves her cigarette back and forth.

"He's my friend. I just don't know if I can give him everything he needs," I try to explain.

"Do you have the sex with him?" she counters.

When I blush and look away, she continues, "So yes. And this sex, is it good?"

"The best," I breathe.

"Is he good man or bad man?"

"He's amazing."

She stamps out her cigarette and rolls her eyes at me. "You love him. The rest is thinking too much."

Is it really that simple? "But what if I'm not good enough for him?"

She reaches out and grabs my chin, holding my face, her eyes locked on mine. "He thinks you are good enough." then shrugs, "Is all that matters."

She leans closer and kisses my forehead before releasing my chin.

When the doorbell rings, she smacks my butt and points to the door.

There's a short bald man with a bouquet of flowers. He's just my height and reminds me of the man on the popcorn box.

"Come on in," I grin.

"You must be Sawyer," he says reaching out his hand. "I'm Tom."

"Nice to meet you, Tom."

"Where's Marie?" he asks, looking past me.

"I'm here," she calls out, walking to join us. "Hello, Tom." She leans down to kiss his cheek and says, "You shouldn't have," when he hands her the flowers.

"They pale in comparison to your beauty."

My eyes widen, and I glance at Marie to check out her reaction. Based on the blush creeping across her cheeks, I'm guessing she likes him.

"Thank you, Tom," she replies in a breathy rasp before turning and going back to the kitchen to put them in a vase.

Tom and I stand awkwardly in the living room until she comes back. She returns with wine for all of us and sits. We follow her lead when she sits. While we wait for dinner to finish baking, she explains my presence to Tom. From the conversation, I glean that Tom lives nearby and has been slowly wooing Marie for some time.

I wonder if her caring for Carmen is what stops her from taking the next step with him. It seems so simple to diagnose problems around me. If only I could do the same for myself. Marie excuses herself to check on Carmen.

I fill the time with small talk. Tom is quite a character, a self-made man. He reminds me of everything I miss about Jared. Not wanting to be rude is the only thing that stops me from calling Jared. I wonder what he's doing, how his day was, and if he's thinking of me at all.

I've gotten so good at extracting myself from physical relationships over the years; it's foreign to me to crave his nearness. In the past, the distance was enough, the thrill of new experiences and people. Have I finally found something that makes all new adventures lose their luster?

Marie returns when the oven buzzer goes off. They're too polite to make me truly feel like the third wheel that I know I am. Once we've finished eating, I excuse myself, claiming exhaustion and retreat to my room to give them space.

Marie ignores my escape attempt and somehow talks me into having some dessert. After a few bites I manage my escape. Their togetherness only enforces my loneliness.

I reach for my phone and call Jared.

"Hey, stranger."

"It hasn't been that long," I argue.

"Feels like it."

"Do you miss me?" I whisper.

"You already know the answer to that," he counters, his voice taking on a husky tone.

"I miss you."

"Come home," he pleads.

Something breaks inside me. I've lived in Denver for years but having Jared tell me to come home, to him, makes me realize how long it's been since I considered a place home.

"As soon as I can. I promise."

"I'll be waiting."

My throat feels thick as I say goodbye, trying my hardest not to cry. He said he'd be waiting. That's a good thing. Why do I feel so emotional over it? I seek solace in sleep.

When I wake up, I open the box, finding old letters from my grandmother to Carmen. With shaking hands, I open the first one. Her handwriting is the same as from her journal, but this letter is nothing like the bullet point list.

This letter is dated September 18, 1971. My father was only ten years old and had broken his arm falling out of a tree. Her love, her fear, her care for my father is so abundantly clear from each word she wrote. Her affection for Carmen is evident as well. She called her "my dearest Carmen" and asked her to come visit.

I read letter after letter, finally being granted a glimpse of the life of not only my father but my grandmother as well. She had been witty, loving, and adventurous in her letters. She was nothing like I remembered her.

By the time my father turned fifteen, the letters began to change. The details were the same, the essentials in written correspondence, the who, what, when, where, and why. The heart was lost, though. The witty remarks that made each letter exude warmth were gone. They were no longer addressed Dearest Carmen, but Dear Carmen.

Something had happened. There were hints in the following letters. In one, she wrote, "I don't feel well." In another, "I'm lost." What had happened to make her feel this way? I avoid the clock next to my bed and the droop of my eyelids as I struggle to read every letter.

The last message has a haunting. "I'm losing my mind," before sleep claims my body. Waking up in unfamiliar places has never bothered me. My internal vagabond embraces it. The only thing that irks me, like an itch I can't reach in the corners of my mind, is her letters. What did she mean she was losing her mind?

I head straight for Carmen's room. Marie is feeding her.

"May I?" I gesture to the bowl of oatmeal in her hands.

She nods, smiling, kissing me on the cheek as she passes it to me. Carmen's eyes soften as I move to sit next to her. I feed her until she slowly lifts one hand and gently shakes her head.

I set the bowl aside, reach for her hand, and hold it in mine. "I've been reading her letters."

"My Agnes," she smiles.

"What happened to her?"

She pinches her eyes shut, and when they reopen, I'm startled to see them wet with tears.

"Her mind."

"I don't understand," I reply gently.

"Keep reading, la mia Sawyer."

I lean forward, kissing her cheek, and get up to let her rest. I will read. I head back to my room, ignoring the grumble of my empty stomach. With each letter, my tension builds, as her hints become full-blown screams. I lift the next letter, its envelope different from all those before it.

I read the return address and gasp, "Nadow View Mental Hospital."

My grandmother spent time in a mental hospital?

chapter 12 ½

Jared

I hang up with Sawyer and fight the impulse to punch something. Her voice, her fucking voice kills me. Why does she have to do this all by herself? I can't help her, and it's the hardest thing I've ever done.

I'm not scheduled to work today, but I decide to head in just to clear my head. The season is winding down. Temperatures have been below freezing overnight so we haven't lost much snow. Our days are numbered, though. Spring is just around the corner, and the resort is gearing up to start their other outdoor activities. Hiking isn't bad, I guess. It's just not boarding.

It's a weekend, end of season, so it's not crowded. I've never liked sharing a lift with a stranger. I lose myself in my thoughts and just let my instincts take over. I know this mountain like the back of my hand. I think back to my first couple of years working here.

I was a wannabe player. A few years back, I used to time it so I'd get on with some hot girl. Majority of them were out-of-towners. It was easy to find someone to hook up with. It was fun until it stopped being that way.

I was having the same conversation repeatedly with the same result every time: some mindless sex for a day or two and then some halfhearted promise to stay in touch once they went home. It was draining. I just couldn't do it anymore.

I went through a hell of a self-imposed dry spell before I met Kristy. Apart from the attraction, I never got what she saw in me. I felt like I was going through the motions the whole time we were together because I just couldn't handle being alone anymore.

When she got pregnant, it only made sense to get married. I just wanted to do the right thing. For a while there, I had the world convinced I was happy. Now I know I was doing my best to try to tell myself I was, because what type of asshole isn't excited to become a father?

When she lost the baby, we both knew. I think she loved me and finally realized it was more than how much I loved her. I liked her, but she deserved better than that. I haven't spoken to her since I was in New Hampshire. She sounded so hopeful on the phone.

Knowing how I feel about Sawyer, I cannot be the type of man to allow another woman to indulge in feelings about me. What she does on her own time is her business, but it would be wrong of me to do anything to encourage her. We shared something awful, something that I will live with the rest of my life; but I've moved on, and she deserves the opportunity to do so as well.

chapter 13

Sawyer

I consume each letter as though they will ease the ache inside me. My grandmother spent six months of 1979 living at Nadow. Something happened between her and my father that prompted her to stay there. What, the letters do not say. It was the year he graduated high school and went on to Dartmouth.

Whatever it was had been enough that for the remainder of his years my father distanced himself from her. She wrote about her treatment with a detached eeriness, considering the horrific treatments she was subjected to. The treatment that seemed most effective at the time was shock therapy. Her letters changed drastically after that. This was the cause of the introduction of the bullet points.

The treatments affected her short and long-term memory. Her coping mechanism became lists. She wrote how her life had dissolved into endless lists, but without them, she would forget to eat, to shower, and to change her clothes.

After I was born, my father tried to repair the distance between them. In one letter, she tells Carmen of the letter she sent my father. He had wanted to bring my mother and me up to New Hampshire to spend the holidays with her. She was terrified that he would figure out something was wrong with her.

She had pushed him away instead, telling him she hadn't wanted to see him, that he had made a mistake getting married so young. Tears blur my vision as I see her admit that that letter broke her heart.

The letter to Carmen telling her that my father died was the worst of all. "Carmen, it has been five days since my Henry died. Each day I forget. Each day my heart breaks when I learn it again. Each time feels like the first time."

When it comes to grief, it's true the pain is always there, but I shake my head trying to imagine the agony of not having the grace of time to dull the first bite of that loss.

"What am I to do with Sawyer? How can I be trusted with a child? I sent her to her godmother for now. What else can I do?"

I feed my fist to my gaping mouthed wail. Marie rushes into my room to wrap her arms around me.

"I didn't know. I didn't know. I didn't know." I rock back and forth in her embrace.

She tries to ask me what happened, what I have read to cause me such pain. I just hold her as she holds me. All these years I just assumed she didn't want me. Why didn't someone tell me along the way?

Once my sobs soften, she pulls away. "I make you some tea."

"Got anything stronger?" I hiccup.

It's still morning, but she returns with a bottle of Jack. I reach for it and take a healthy gulp, gasping as it burns down my throat. I gulp down another shot before I set the bottle down on the floor next to the bed.

"Why are you crying?" she demands.

I shake my head. "All this time I thought my grandmother didn't want me."

She gently bends down to grasp the neck of the bottle and helps herself to a gulp before setting it on the dresser across from the bed. She walks back over to me, smacking me softly to make more room for her to sit next to me.

Once she's settled next to me, her arm drapes around my shoulders. "What made you think this? Did your grandmother give you to the state? No, she did not. She sent you to Carmen, to a good school. This does not sound like someone with no love."

I nod, seeing the truth in her words. "I felt abandoned so I reacted in anger. I've been so angry, for so long. I feel ashamed."

She holds me tightly as I cry on her shoulder. "Now you know. You must never question this again. You deserve love and have been loved."

Carmen deserves better than I am. She was the woman who raised me to be strong, passionate, and giving. When I graduated, I left. I knew Carmen loved me, but I let my own feelings of inadequacy push me away from her. I took off, so certain that I didn't need anyone or anything.

"I shouldn't have left Carmen the way I did," I confess.

"Shh." She pushes my hair from my eyes. "When the baby bird takes flight, the mama is never more proud."

"I should have—"

"You are here now."

I nod, and she stands so I can get up and spend time with the woman my grandmother trusted to raise me. She is lucid when I go to sit with her.

"I saw myself as a burden."

She gently shakes her head. "You are a gift."

I bite back a sob as my eyes well. "I'm so sorry I lost contact with you."

When her lips pull up in her familiar smile, I'm pulled back in time. She was Sophia Loren to me, even now. "La mia Sawyer."

"La mia Carmen." I hold her hand in both of mine.

Marie watches us, leans up against the doorway, and says, "Tell her about your love."

I blink at her, and she winks at me. "Your man."

Carmen's eyes have moved to Marie and come back to rest on mine. If I didn't know better, I could swear they were twinkling.

"A love?"

Why does telling Carmen finally make it feel real? "Yes." I can't help the smile that comes with thinking of Jared.

Marie encourages me to talk about him as Carmen listens on, rapt.

"His name is Jared. He's the boy I spent summers with when I wasn't at school. He is the best man I've ever known. I've been awful, and he doesn't care. He just loves me. Part of me doesn't feel like I deserve him."

She pulls her hand from my grasp to set it over both of my arms and squeeze. "Go to him."

"What?" I blink. "I'm here with you, for you. I can't leave you."

She presses her other hand to her heart. "You never left me."

Marie is next to me, pulling me. "Go pack."

"But—" I look back at Carmen as Marie tugs me into the hallway.

"She doesn't want you to see her go," she explains.

She is so giving, even to the end. Carmen doesn't want me to watch her die. She wants me to go make amends with Jared. I nod; my eyes filling with tears again as I blindly shove my clothes back into my suitcase.

If there was ever a life lesson staring me in the face, this is it; be unselfish with your love. Spread it all around.

Carmen loved me enough to let me go all those years ago. She didn't hold my need to find my own way against me. She only rejoiced in my finding my way back to her.

I know I'm not done learning exactly why my grandmother pushed me away. There are letters I still need to read, but I have time for that. I'm also lucky enough to have the love of a generous man who will hold my hand as I do it. Marie offers to drive my rental and me to the airport. It will be an excuse to call Tom and have him come pick her up.

She busies herself calling him while I take a quick shower. I can hear her from the hallway as I go to say goodbye to Carmen. I swallow the emotions rising in my throat, as I know this will probably be the last time I see her.

She smiles quietly, her serene beauty still stronger than her failing body.

"I can't thank you enough for everything. I am who am I today because I had an amazing woman to look up to. I love you so much, Carmen." The tears I tried so hard to hold back push their way through and stream down my face.

"I'm so sorry I left the way I did."

Her hand cups my cheek, drying some of my tears. "La mia Sawyer. You never left me."

"La mia Carmen," I choke.

She pulls my hand to her lips to kiss it, and then I kiss her cheeks. I may always regret the time I lost with her, but my heart feels full in knowing she never held that against me. People put value in objects, possessions. Just seeing her again, telling her I'm sorry, feels like a gift.

For so long, I ignored the love given freely to me. In my own twisted interpretation, I took the actions of one individual to define what I thought I deserved.

Carmen is asleep by the time Marie and I need to leave. Careful not to disturb her, I give her one last gentle kiss before I go. Tom is parked on the street waiting so he can follow my rental. I return his wave, smiling. Marie blows him a kiss, making him blush right to the top of his baldhead.

"I like Tom," I whisper, sliding into my seat.

She fluffs her hair, her mouth stretching into a grin. "He is a good man."

Marie and Tom stay with me until I've finished returning the rental. Saying goodbye to Marie becomes a full body event, and she clasps me to her chest. I thank her. She opened her heart to me these past few days. I feel a sense of relief that Carmen has her. That she isn't alone.

They leave me, Marie winking at me one last time over her shoulder as they walk away hand in hand.

I manage to land a standby seat on the next flight to Denver. I decide against calling Jared, wanting to surprise him. I'm still reeling from everything I've learned about my grandmother, but somehow the thought of seeing Jared, of feeling his arms around me again, leaves me feeling giddier than anything else does.

I luck out on a seat near an outlet and plug my phone in. I have to talk to someone, so I call Sarah.

"Hey, Sawyer," Will answers her phone.

"Hiya, Price. Where's Sarah?"

"She's upstairs. I'm walking you up to her right now."

"Cool. Thanks." I pull my legs up into my seat and cross them. "So how've you been?"

"Good. Busy. End of the nine weeks is approaching so I need to get grades loaded. Otherwise, just doing some stuff around the house. I'll let my lovely wife fill you in on that." I hear him call out to her, letting her know I'm on the phone.

"It was nice hearing your voice, Will," I say, before he passes the phone to her, "Keep taking good care of my girl."

I hear what sounds like a soft kiss. "It's my life's mission. Bye, Sawyer."

"Hey, babe." I can hear her smile through the phone.

It makes me miss her.

"I love you," I blurt.

"I love you too, Sawyer. Is everything okay? You sound…" She trails off.

"You ever feel like everything you thought you knew was wrong?" I ask.

"Um, yes. Just look at Will and me."

She's right. She was so sure he couldn't love her and ran the first time their young love was tested. She had an excuse, though. Eighteen year olds are not known for their decision-making skills under pressure. That comes with age and maturity. She and Will are so solid now; I think they needed to grow up and find themselves first.

What's my excuse? I've been hanging onto this shield over my heart forever. The only reason Jared and I still have a chance is because of how patient and stubborn he has been in allowing me to face my fear of letting someone love me. For so long, I've convinced myself that there was something so fundamentally wrong with me that I didn't deserve love.

"My grandmother didn't have me live with her because she had mental health issues. She was scared she wouldn't be able to take care of me. She," I gulp, "sent me away because she loved me."

"Oh, honey."

I refuse to cry again, especially sitting at a crowded airport gate. Sarah, the best friend a girl could ever ask for, cries for me. She, throughout the years, has come closest to knowing my deepest fears of inadequacy. She always built me back up, never letting me dwell in negativity without trying so hard to make me believe I deserved love.

Sarah was the first person from whom I accepted unconditional love. Without her, I don't know where I would be today. When we met, I was all bravado, and she was hurting. Over the years, we've reversed roles more times than I can count. If Jared is the love of my life, Sarah is the sister I never had.

She keeps talking, "I knew there had to be some reason. I knew it."

She did. She always argued my grandmother must have had a reason for sending me away. I just chose to believe it was something to do with me and never opened myself up to the possibility it was *for* me.

"So…" Silence. "Jared?"

"I'm going home right now."

"Have you told him anything yet?"

I shake my head then laugh at myself, remembering she can't see me. "Not yet. You don't think he might change his mind about me, do you?"

"Are you kidding me? That boy loves you, loves you. Don't even consider the alternative. You need to allow yourself to let him love you."

"I'll try," I reply softly.

"That's all you can do. Trust me. It's worth it."

When I hear my name called to the gate agent, I tell Sarah I love her again and promise to talk more once I'm back in Denver. At the gate, I get the good news. A seat opened up, and I'm now officially going home.

While waiting in line to board the plane, I text Petey to see if he can pick me up from the airport. I smile down at his immediate response. With any luck, I'll be home before Jared gets off work.

I have my whole flight to think of what I'll say, of how I'll ask Jared for his forgiveness in my keeping him at arm's length.

Once we've landed and I turn the corner to head toward baggage claim, I know I've been had.

Strong arms lift me as Jared crushes me to his chest. "Heard you needed a lift," he grins before molding his lips to mine.

People shuffle around us as he takes his time saying hello. Everything I had convinced myself I needed to say on the plane seems pointless now. He doesn't need words. He just wants me. I haven't even been gone from him that long, but his kiss reminds me of how much I miss the way he tastes, the way he smells, the way his arms feel wrapped around me.

I could stand here all day. I'm sad, briefly, when he sets me back down. The only thing keeping me from pulling his lips back down to mine is my knowing that as soon as we get back to the condo, it won't be just his lips on me.

I don't argue his driving us back. He has to look at the road while I get to look at him. Finally deciding to love him back, to accept his love, has released a girl from inside of me that I didn't know existed. She's happy, totally and completely happy.

Every smile I smiled before this moment feels like practice. Self-awareness raises her unsure head, and my grin falters a fraction.

"Don't." Jared is so tuned into me. "I love your smile."

Like a burner cranked to high, the intense joy within is back, full force. I've never been so relieved that Petey is a meddling fool. I will have to think of some way to thank him for getting Jared to come get me.

It's another realization of the love I've ignored all around me. I've been such an idiot. What I could have lost if I had succeeded in pushing him away dawns on me. Now I finally recognize the truth of how empty my life would be without him.

I squeeze his hand, drawing his eyes to mine. "I love you."

His eyes widen in surprise. "What'd you say?"

I smile until it hurts. "I love you, Jared Keller."

He groans, swerving to pull off the road.

"What are you doing?" I gasp.

His SUV is in park, my seatbelt has been unbuckled, and I am hauled into his lap before I know it.

His hands are in my hair as he pulls my lips down to his. I feel the rapid drumming of his heart beating through his clothes as I steady myself against his chest.

"You don't get to say that without me getting to kiss you," he murmurs against my mouth.

"I love you," I answer, tasting him.

He groans again, "I love you so much, Sawyer."

I lift my head, pulling back slightly. "Please, take me home so I can show you just how much I love you."

He tips his head back, closing his eyes until it rests on the headrest. I suppress my giggle at his obvious arousal. I've never felt more wanted, loved, cherished. I just wish it wasn't on the side of a highway.

I kiss his closed eyelids before slipping back into my seat. We're back on the road, gravel flying in our wake the moment my seatbelt clicks into place.

There has been some speculation that I am somewhat of an aggressive driver. I'm not technically admitting to anything. However, Jared is driving like a man possessed. I love it. Seeing him, my gentle giant, so bordering out of control is the hottest thing I've ever witnessed.

He wants me. He wants me badly. It's a heady rush. He does a craptastic-parking job when we get home. There is a serious possibility his SUV will be towed, but neither of us cares. Force of habit is the only thing that reminds us even to close the doors before we dash upstairs. Once inside, our four hands work to strip us of anything keeping his skin from mine.

Clothes are in the foyer, kitchen, hallway, and finally he divests me of my boy shorts once we reach my room. I'm lifted, flying, coasting, landing softly against my pillows, his body following. We roll, sliding against each other, trying somehow to touch every inch of our bodies before anything else. My body is humming with need, each stroke only intensifying it.

"Jared." I border on begging.

"I want you so bad," he whispers against my neck.

"I'm right here," I pant.

"I missed touching you. I need to feel you," he confesses, kissing his way down one arm.

"Please." I lift my hips; the ache for him to fill me is almost painful.

His arms band around my waist, and he drags his fingertips down my legs. My fingers scrape my scalp as I bury them in my hair. I can't handle it anymore. He's reached the end of his control as well. My eyes drift open, and I part my legs wider when I feel the tip of his erection tease me.

"Jared," I moan as he sinks inch by glorious inch into me.

Once he's as deep as he can go, once there is no possible negative space around us, I exhale. With that breath, I release every negative thing I ever told myself, every impulse I've ever had to feel that I'm not deserving of love.

This man, this amazing man I've known over half of my life, is giving me all of himself now. He has been patiently and sometimes not so patiently, waiting for me to figure my shit out. He has met me more than halfway repeatedly. I'd be an idiot to let fear keep me from gobbling up every part of him.

He gave me space without abandoning me. Now that I've exorcised the demons of my own creation, I'm ready to give him all of me. Our lovemaking is a contradiction in itself, passionate pounding of limbs one moment to subtle savoring of each infinitesimal movement.

The simple twist of his hips as he pushes impossibly further into me flips a switch inside me. I don't crash or fall, I detonate, exploding into uncountable pieces and somehow reforming into something brand new. I bare my soul to Jared and find my mate.

I never want to be without him again.

I hardly have a chance to recover before his entire body tenses around me, over me, inside me. With my name on his lips, he comes hard. Fucking sexiest thing I've ever seen. He lowers his lips to mine before turning on his side and pulling me to his chest. We kiss slowly, tenderly, as we cherish each other.

I should be terrified. In my head, I recognize how scary it is to love someone so much. It's a loss of control. It's the choice to trust him forever with my heart. Even knowing this, I've never felt safer or more certain.

chapter 13 ½

Jared

Sawyer loves me. I knew she did. I just never expected her to admit it aloud.

She's always been a less talk more action type of girl, unless she's giving someone grief. I've had her love as a friend for years. This is different. We both know it. I fully intend to tease her at some point in the future over the fact that I figured it out first.

Lying here, with her in my arms, I know it's time for her to get all the shit that's been dragging her down, off her chest. I kiss her temple, leaving my lips there so I can smell her conditioner and feel the tickle of her pulse against my mouth.

"I missed you so much," she sighs, stepping her fingertips slowly up my arm.

"You happy to see me?" I joke.

Her mumbled affirmation makes me grin.

"I never want to leave this bed," she adds, pressing against me.

I tighten my arms around her. "Be careful what you wish for."

Half a laugh erupts before she takes a shaky breath. "This is better than anything I could have ever wished for."

I lift my head, my eyes searching her face. Her words are light, but coated in a sadness she can't hide from me.

"What's wrong?"

She starts blinking like crazy and tries to pull away, but I don't let her. She pinches her eyes shut as I stare. She gulps.

"I was so wrong about her, Jared," she swallows again. "So wrong," her voice breaks.

"I don't understand. What happened?"

I sit, pulling her into my lap.

"She was sick, even institutionalized at one point. She did shock therapy; and basically, she had no short-term memory. That's why her journal read the way it did."

One tear escapes, and I brush it from her cheek. "I'm so sorry, babe."

I can't even imagine what learning that did to her. She was so sure there was something lacking in herself to consider anything else.

"I failed her, Jared." She shakes her head. "I never even tried to see her or get to know her."

My hands travel up and down the slope of her back as I try to comfort her. "You didn't know."

More tears escape as she tucks her face into the curve of my neck. "And Carmen, I left her without even looking back. What kind of person does that make me?"

I lean back, bringing one hand to lift her chin until her eyes are locked on mine. "You're not a bad person. You were young and wanted to find your own way. Did either of them come after you?"

She shakes her head, so I continue, "You didn't do anything wrong. You are one of the most giving, selfless people I know."

She gives me a wet smile, so I drop my hand and pull her back to my chest. She's stubborn, so I'm positive this won't be the only time we have this conversation.

I decide now might be a smart time to confess what I've been up to while she was gone.

chapter 14

Sawyer

My mouth drops. "You did what?"

He looks terrified for a moment and hesitates, but I cut him off. "You bought my grandmother's house?"

He cringes, nodding, and I crush my lips to his. "You are the most amazing man in the whole world."

His shoulders sag, and he grins against my lips. "Thank fuck. I thought you were going to be pissed at me."

"But how did you do it? I saw the closing paperwork. I'm pretty sure I would have noticed your name."

He scratches the back of his head, his shirt lifting to expose his taut stomach. "I managed to find the buyer and talk her into selling it to me. Once she heard about you and what I was trying to do she agreed."

I pull back, almost asking him why he would do that for me, but I already know the answer. It would have freaked me out a couple of days ago. I wouldn't have reacted well at all. My anger at her would have transferred over to him.

"I love you." I dive back into our kiss.

He bought my grandmother's house, the place my father grew up in and the place I never had an opportunity to grow to love.

"Do you want to live there?" I ask.

He shrugs. "Maybe someday. I just couldn't shake the feeling you belonged there when we were there."

"But the studio?" I pout.

"We can rent the house out or just keep it as a place we'll vacation to."

"Are you loaded? That house was not cheap."

He waggles his eyebrows at me. "Only with me for my money?"

I push on his shoulder, and he leans in to nip at my lip. "I want to know."

"I had a little bit of cash but not enough to buy it outright. The rest is mortgaged."

I groan, "I don't want you to be in debt because of me. Let me pay the difference."

He smirks. "Woman."

I open my mouth to argue, but he silences me with his finger. "Let me do this for you."

I sneak my tongue out and lick the pad of his finger, my heart racing as I watch his gaze turn molten.

Pressing gently on his chest, I push him back down to the bed and he falls, moving his finger from my mouth.

Lining myself over him, I descend slowly, sinking until he fills me. "I'll have to think of some way to pay you back."

His hands slide up to grip my hips. "No payback needed," he whispers.

I swivel my hips and pull back an inch before easing back down, and his eyes roll back.

"You like this, Jared?" I tease.

His grip tightens, fingers biting into my skin as he lifts me before driving his hips upward, simultaneously slamming me down onto him. "I fucking love this," he answers.

I surrender to him, falling forward enough to brace my hands on his chest as he pounds me from below. My body is his to command. It's a level of open trust, built on freely giving and receiving his love. He loves me gently with every sweet thing he does to make me happy; but at the same time, he can turn me on and make me feel like a sexual goddess.

I trust him enough to lose control with him and know he will never do anything to hurt me. I lift my eyes to watch his face. He is so fucking hot. Beads of sweat gather at his hairline. He opens his eyes and pauses when he sees me watching him.

I drop until my chest is flat on his. He lifts his head to capture my lips. He slows but somehow his hips continue their beautifully torturous assault on me, shifting from frantic to leisurely. This time, a gentle warmth expands within me until I crest and pulse deep inside. Jared is unable to hold out. He follows me with a groan.

Carmen passed away today. Part of me knew it even before Marie called. Something just felt not right all day. I was at the studio, and even though I should have been feeling nothing but contentment at the upcoming opening, something was off.

I decide against bothering Jared with it at work. While he works year-round at the resort, today is the last official day of the ski season. I can see him, clear as day, probably boarding in a t-shirt right now.

One moment the world was clinging desperately to the last vestiges of winter, then almost overnight, spring asserted herself dramatically. Everything feels bright and green.

"Jared's here," is all the notice I get before he turns the corner and steps into my office.

"What are you doing here?" I ask, surprised but so happy to see him.

"Hey." He catches me as I hurl myself into his arms. "Thought I'd surprise you. Everything okay?"

I shake my head against his neck. "Carmen passed away."

His hand slides up to cup the back of my head as he pulls me closer.

I cling to him, mourning the woman who was the closest thing I had to a mother after mine had passed away. He reaches behind him to close the door of my office before walking me over to a loveseat I have against one wall.

He murmurs sweet declarations in my ear, how much he loves me, how she knew I loved her, and how happy he was that I had her. I blink up at him when he offers to go with me to her funeral.

Knowing without a doubt how I feel about him has changed Jared. He has no problem confidently swooping in to take care of me. I might fuss at him, but it doesn't stop him. I trust him, and he knows I'll do the same for him.

After I've calmed down, he takes me home. I sit on the couch and watch him, laptop in hand, book our flights after he talks to Marie. I'm still sad. There's an ache inside my chest knowing I won't see Carmen again.

With the studio opening, we are only staying there two days. Even though Marie graciously offered to have us stay with her, we decide to stay at a nearby hotel instead. I don't want her to feel obligated to take care of us, and I know if we stay with her, she will.

Jared is my hero. He takes charge of everything and allows me the space to grieve without even having to worry if I packed underwear or not. He probably packed ridiculous ones that are more for taking off than for comfort; but still, it's one less thing to think about. He coordinates calls with John and with Catherine to ensure everything will be ready for us to open our doors when we get home.

We dress somberly for the flight and drive directly to Marie's home from the airport. There is a memorial tonight, and the funeral is tomorrow. I am able to hold back my tears until we get to her house. Once she pulls me into her arms, I'm lost. She smells like Carmen. I never stood a chance.

She blatantly observes Jared and kisses both of his cheeks, silently giving her approval. There's a small group of friends and family members already here. We circulate slowly, offering our condolences. I slip away after a bit, letting Jared know before I do that I just need a moment to myself. I find myself in her room, staring at the now empty bed.

It feels like no time has passed from the last time I saw her. An overwhelming sense of gratitude that I was able to see her one last time washes over me. I can't imagine how heartbroken I would have felt if I hadn't had that chance. I get how lucky I am to have said goodbye.

I make my way back to Jared to let him know I'm back before finding Marie and offering to help. She puts me to work arranging some food on the dining room table. Jared comes to keep me company and help until all of the food is out. We stay longer than we planned.

Marie and Tom sit close together, sweetly holding hands. Jared and I seem to mirror them. I hope for her sake they stop dancing around each other and just move in together. She's strong, she's independent, but there's no reason for either of them to be alone when it's clear how much they care about one another.

I wonder if people ever saw Jared and me as a couple. I know Will had his theories when he stayed in the condo last summer. In no time, it will be a year since they reunited. The older I get, the faster time seems to pass. When my eyelids start drooping, Jared says our goodbyes and takes me to the hotel.

We strip, tired and emotional. We don't make love but still find our way into each other's arms. I was never a cuddler before Jared, but now I find myself needing some sort of skin contact with him to sleep. We wake refreshed but still emotionally subdued.

The cemetery is not far from Marie's neighborhood. The Arizona sun is brutal despite the early time. There are white tents set up in an effort to block out some of the heat. We stand not far from Marie and Tom. Carmen was Catholic. Her priest speaks briefly about her and what a wonderful woman she was.

I smile, agreeing with everything he says and once again feeling lucky to have known and loved her. I only wish I hadn't missed the opportunity to say goodbye to my grandmother. Once her casket is lowered and most of the other attendees have left, we go to say goodbye to Marie.

She holds me tightly, thanking me for bringing Carmen peace in her final days. I am overwhelmed and feel undeserving of her gratitude. She was the one who made sure Carmen never wanted for anything in the end. I have lost Carmen, and for that I will always be sad, but I can't help the joy I feel in having the opportunity to meet Marie.

We part as friends, and I know we will forever remain that way.

We are back in the air and flying home to Denver that same afternoon. I should be amped up over the studio opening, but I'm not. I've devoted so much time and energy to this project in the hope that it would fill a piece of me I felt was missing.

I'm not sure why, but I feel pulled to New Hampshire.

I turn to Jared. "Have you given any more thought to what you would like to do with my grandmother's house?"

He pulls my hand into his lap, squeezing it. "I told you to stop calling it that. It's our house now. I'm open to whatever you want to do."

I clear my throat. "Would you consider moving there?" I pause. "I know your job, your dad—"

He cuts me off with a kiss. "Do you want to move to New Hampshire?"

I blink. "It would be crazy. The studio is about to—"

He stops me again with a shake of his head. "Sawyer, none of that other stuff matters. Just think about it. Do you want to move there?"

I bite my lips and nod.

He leans down to kiss me. "Then we'll move."

"It's not that simple," I argue.

He shrugs. "It can be. You can trust Catherine to run the studio. You know she'd be thrilled with the challenge."

He's right. "Are you serious? You'll do this?"

He smiles. "There are mountains there too. It'd probably take more to convince me if it was somewhere like Florida. As long as there's snow, I'm happy."

"Sarah is going to freak out," I giggle. "But," I pause, becoming more serious, "there's something I want to do first."

chapter 14 ½

Jared

I'm on the farm where Sawyer grew up, in the orchard of trees she used to climb; the place where her parents are buried. We flew to New Hampshire first to meet with the estate attorney. There was one final thing to settle her grandmother's estate: her remains.

Not long after Carmen's funeral, Sawyer started wearing that ring we found in her grandmother's, well, our house. She wears it as a reminder not to repeat the mistake her grandmother made. Sawyer is so deserving of the love we all have for her. The ring helps remind her not to push people away.

Sawyer wants to bring her grandmother here so that she'll rest with Sawyer's mom and dad. She explained there weren't any remains of her parents to bury; but she had been so moved by the headstone Beau's parents got, she considers this place to be their final resting place.

Sawyer had a matching headstone made for her grandmother to stand beside the one for her mom and dad. Half of her remains will be buried here, the other half back in New Hampshire.

We've started the move but nothing is unpacked yet. The house is so big it will be years before we've filled it. For now, we've decided just to live on the ground floor. We'll branch out to the rest of the house in time.

Today is all about her grandmother. People who love Sawyer have come to support her as she says goodbye to the grandmother she never really knew. Her headstone simply reads:

Agnes Sterling

Full of love in her
own way

We are here today for Sawyer. We are here because we love her and are proud of the person she is. She is here to accept that, though she will never fully understand why her grandmother didn't tell Sawyer about her condition, she did indeed love her.

Sawyer has never been very religious. She faces us; momentarily wringing her hands before she straightens her shoulders, and clears her throat.

"Thank you all for coming today. It means so much to me that you would do that for me. Some of you never even met my grandmother." She smiles at Sarah, Will, and their parents.

"Some of you only met her briefly, like me." She nods toward Bess, Beau and his parents, Lynn and Joe.

"Without her, I wouldn't be where I am today. I didn't understand the choices she made when she made them, but I've had the opportunity to understand them better now. I hope she knows, wherever she is, how grateful I am for the sacrifices she made. I only hope she has found peace. I think being near my mom and dad," she glances up at the blossoming fruit trees behind us, "in this beautiful place, she will be able to rest."

We each hold a flower, and once she's done talking, go one by one to set it in front of her headstone. I wait at the end, with two extra bouquets for her parents' headstone. Sawyer quirks an eyebrow up at me, but she doesn't say anything when I don't lay my flowers down.

Once everyone starts to head back to the main house, I stop Sawyer, asking her to hang back with me for a minute. I hold her hand, walk back to her parents' headstone, and move to stand Sawyer beside it.

I look up and take a deep breath. "Mr. and Mrs. Sterling, I've come here today with Sawyer to introduce myself. I'm only sorry I never got a chance to meet you both. The thing is I'm in love with your daughter."

I look up, locking eyes with her and see hers filled with tears. I hold my hand out to her, and she tucks herself into my side as we both look down at their gravestone.

I kiss the top of her pretty, pink head and go on, "I'd like to spend the rest of my life with her."

Her mouth drops. "Your daughter is a bit of a rebel. She has mixed feelings about marriage, but I'd like to try and talk her into a commitment ceremony." I hear her watery giggle beside me. "Thing is I'd like to ask for your blessing."

I set the bouquets down gently before reaching out to rest my hand on the cool stone.

"How will we know if they've given you their blessing?" Sawyer asks, looking up at me.

I give her a tight smile and pull her hand to my heart. "We'll know it right here. I swear to you, I will do everything in my power to cherish you for the rest of my life. I love you, Sawyer."

She nods, using her hand to brush the tears from her eyes. "I'm sure they'd give you their blessing. I love you too, Jared Keller."

epilogue

Jared

One year later

It's our not a wedding-wedding day. While fully supportive of anyone else's desire to have a wedding, Sawyer is weirded out by the whole "our love is defined by a piece of paper" thing. I'm piece of paper neutral. I really don't care as long as she's happy.

This is our happy medium. We're making an official commitment to each other in front of all of our friends and family. We're living full time in the New Hampshire house now.

Sawyer hesitated initially in turning the studio over to Catherine. Once we settled in, our ever growing love for this magical home made our decision to move that much easier. So now, on this thankfully sunny, spring day, in the backyard of the house her father grew up in, we're making it unofficially, official.

My dad is the only one still pushing for a traditional marriage. He should know by now my girl is one of a kind. My mom, who is nontraditional in her own right, has been nothing but supportive.

Sawyer and Sarah planned the whole thing. We aren't having someone officiate, but Will is standing up with me, and Sarah with Sawyer. The backyard is decorated similar to a wedding setup, with chairs and a wooden vine-covered trellis for us to stand under.

The trellis is set up right in front of a stone memorial bench for her grandmother. Sawyer never had an opportunity to know her grandmother. For too many years, Sawyer fed into the notion that it was because there was something wrong with herself. We know now that under some misguided fear of hurting her, Sawyer's grandmother had distanced herself to protect Sawyer.

Sawyer makes a point to spend time with her grandmother every week. We spread her remaining ashes beneath the bench. Sawyer talks to her, tells her about her day, her hopes and dreams, and bitches about me sometimes. That's my girl. She can make something beautiful out of sorrow. She's choosing to make new memories rooted in love.

I don't need anyone to remind me how lucky I am to spend the rest of my life with her.

"Ready?"

I turn to Will and grin. "Born ready."

He shakes his head, but I know he understands. We've become good friends since that summer he followed Sarah out to Denver. It sucks that we weren't able to talk them into moving closer. In fact, they both looked at us as though we were crazy but promised an extended visit every summer.

They live in Georgia and love it. At least we're closer than we had been before, and Sawyer's thrilled about being in the same time zone as her best friend. In addition, we're now closer to the farm where she grew up. Beau seems like a great guy. I can tell Sawyer is thrilled to have him back in her life. As long as she's happy, I'm good.

Will and I walk out of the side door as Sawyer and Sarah come from the back door. This one part of the ceremony was important to Sawyer. She didn't want me just waiting there for her at the end of an aisle. I could argue that I'm used to waiting for her, but the symbolism of what she was going for is sweet, so I have kept my mouth shut.

She wanted us to meet each other halfway. I walk on the left side of the seated guests while she walks along the right. I'm not surprised she isn't wearing a traditional wedding dress, but she still looks like the most beautiful women in the world.

Her dress has a retro feel to it, with a high waist and a poufy skirt. The color is a pale mint that works with her loose pink curls. She is, as always, the most beautiful woman I have ever seen. Every couple of steps, I catch her eyes. She covers her mouth and laughs when I'm so busy looking at her, I bump into one of the end chairs.

"Sorry, dude." I pat someone's shoulder and I keep moving toward her.

By the time we reach each other, I can't wait to touch her. I cup her cheeks and dip my mouth to hers. Our friends and family laugh but aren't surprised. When I open my eyes and find hers have gone all soft, I just want to kiss her again.

"Hey, babe," I whisper.

She squeezes her grip on my arms and replies, "Hey, lover."

I groan. Fuck; that sounds sexy. Sarah clears her throat loudly, and we both glance at her. She presses her lips together, and keeping her face toward us, glances in the direction of all of our guests.

Right. I reach out for Sawyer's hand and squeeze it when she slips it into mine. Together, we turn to face our family and friends.

"Thank you all for coming to join us today."

"It means so much to us that you are all here," Sawyer continues.

I turn to look at her and reach for her other hand.

"I love you more than I ever knew was possible, Jared Keller. With you, I have found the freedom to find myself. With your love, I am many things. I am strong, I am brave, and I am loved." She pauses, moving our joined hands to rest on her perfectly rounded belly. "With your love, I am also going to be a mother. I can't wait to spend the rest of my life on this adventure with you."

I lift one hand to smooth away the wetness gathering at the corner of her eye.

"Sawyer Sterling, I love you so much. I only have myself to give you, but I'm yours. Everything that makes me who I am I give to you. I'll spend the rest of my life doing anything I can to make you smile. You and I, Sawyer. Forever." I drop my lips to hers again before kneeling to place one more kiss on her stomach.

The End

acknowledgements

The creation process of writing a book is not unlike what I experienced physically while pregnant with my two kids. I gained weight, I struggled to sleep, I was at times a grouchy bear to be around, and I cried frequently. I'd like to acknowledge and thank my family for still loving me after 7 books.

To my closest author friends, Melissa Collins (my wife), Jennifer Berg (my mistress), Renee Carlino (my lover), and Lisa Paul (my hooker), you keep me sane and support me is ways that I'll never be able to fully repay. My betas, Amy, Nasha, Evette, Nicola, Jennifer, Renee, Jessica, Rachel, and Michelle; thank you so much for helping me make Sawyer Says the story I dreamed of telling.

To Yesenia Vargas and the team at Hot Tree Editing, thank you for making sure I dotted all my i's, crossed all my t's and translating my gibberish. To Sarah Hansen with Okay Creations, thank you for another beautiful cover. To Tami with Integrity Formatting, thank you for making the insides of my books so pretty. To Kris and the team at Red Coat Pr, thank you for helping readers find me.

For every amazingly supportive and wonderful blog that has helped me along the way. Whenever you shared a pic, or a link, commented on a post, made a teaser, and told your readers about my books you made my success possible. Thank you from the bottom of my heart for everything that you do.

about the author

New York Times and USA Today bestselling author with six books out and many more to come. She was born and raised in Alexandria, Virginia. Ever the mild-mannered citizen, Carey spends her days working in the world of finance, and at night, she retreats into the lives of her fictional characters. Supporting her all the way are her husband, three sometimes-adorable children, and their nine-pound attack Yorkie.

I'd love to hear from you!

info@careyheywood.com

www.careyheywood.com

Other Books Available everywhere

Better

Her

Him

Stages of Grace

Uninvolved

A Bridge of Her Own

Coming July 2014

By Carey Heywood

Book 1 in Carolina Days Series
The Other Side of Someday

Falling in love? Courtney Grayson has been there, done that.

Men, who needs them? Love wasn't everything she thought it would be. This time around she's doing things differently. She hasn't sworn off men for good, just isn't interested in settling. Trusting someone with her heart again? Someday, but not today.

Falling in love? Sorry, Clay Bradshaw is not the guy for you.

He's never been in love and he doesn't see it happening. Hooking up can be fun, but more often than not, women are a distraction he doesn't need. He's a busy man, and doesn't have time to date, let alone fall in love. Will someone ever change that? There's always a chance, someday.

Life doesn't always go as planned, and love may find them both on the other side of someday.

Look for these other great reads:

MELISSA COLLINS

Let Love
BE

BOOK 4 IN *THE LOVE* SERIES

Let Love Be by Melissa Collins

What would bring you happiness in a world that was suddenly empty?

For Lucy Crane, the answer is simple: her daughter. When her husband is killed in a tragic accident, Lucy loses her desire to live, but only one thing keeps her going – her unborn daughter. Focusing on being a mother helps Lucy cope with her loss, but kids grow up and they leave home, eventually. Eighteen years after losing her first and only love, Lucy is faced with the opportunity to find the happiness for which she's always longed. Her own fears become her worst enemies as she learns how to embrace love once again.

Evan Donovan is also facing his own struggles. Forced to retire from the FDNY because of lung damage caused by 9/11, Evan moves to upstate New York where he hopes to find a little peace and quiet. Old habits die hard, and Evan's hero complex and survivor's guilt constantly remind him of how difficult it is to be vulnerable. But for the first time in his life, he's tired of being alone.

Drawing strength from one another, Lucy and Evan discover how beautiful it is to let love be a part of their lives.

ready for you

A second chance at first love.

USA *Today* Bestselling Author

J.L. BERG

Ready for You by J.L. Berg

Eight years ago, Garrett Finnegan's world shattered the day Mia vanished from his life. He's been struggling to pick up the pieces ever since. Haunted by memories and ghosts of the past, he chooses a solitary existence rather than risk his heart again.

Mia Emerson has made one wrong decision after another but none worse than walking away from the boy who stole her heart so long ago. When her new life is turned upside down, she finds herself returning to her roots and the hometown she left behind. Maybe now she can find a way to heal from the devastating mistakes of her past.

When a chance encounter brings these former lovers together, passion reignites in a way neither is prepared for. Can Garrett move beyond his anger and find a way to forgive? Will Mia's insecurities and fears cause her to once again flee the life she's destined to live?

It only took
a moment to
change her
entire life . . .

Nowhere
but Here

RENÉE
CARLINO

USA Today Bestselling
Author of *Sweet Thing*

a novel

ATRIA
UNBOUND

Nowhere But Here by Renee Carlino

A Chicago reporter in her mid-twenties unexpectedly finds love in Napa Valley when she's assigned to spend a week with a famously reclusive genius.

Kate Corbin has lost her spark. From the outside, her life seems charmed. She has a handsome, long-term boyfriend and a budding journalism career at a popular Chicago newspaper. But in reality, her relationship is going nowhere, and she's quickly losing motivation for what she once believed was her dream job. When her boyfriend dumps her unceremoniously, Kate loses all hope of finding love.

With no living family and few friends, Kate confides in her boss. Trusting that the hungry, ace reporter is buried somewhere deep inside, he gives Kate the opportunity to jumpstart her career. The assignment: to interview the famously reclusive R.J. Lawson, a wealthy tech genius who disappeared years ago but recently reemerged as a Napa Valley vintner. The week takes an unexpected turn, however, when Lawson refuses to divulge any information. Desperate for a lead, Kate turns to Jamie, a vineyard hand who shows her the romance of wine country— and stirs her aching heart. But his connection to Lawson is ambiguous, and when Jamie disappears before the end of the week, Kate is left to investigate another story: the truth behind the man who stole her heart.

STORM FRONT

BOOK TWO

THE CHARISTOWN SERIES

Lisa N. Paul

Storm Front by Lisa N. Paul

The Darker the Storm, The Deeper the Pain...

Love knows no bounds when two people are destined to be together. One fights to maintain the distance; while the other battles to close the gap.

The Brighter the Light at the End...

Will they move forward together or finally close the last remaining door to their past?

It's time for Ryan and Ashley to decide. But once that decision is made, there will be no going back...

Always Reach for the Light...

A Neighborhood bar where old wounds heal, friends become family, and some...become lovers...

Danny's on Main is where their story continues... Where they all shelter each other during the...

Storm Front

www.ingramcontent.com/pod-product-compliance
Lightning Source LLC
Chambersburg PA
CBHW070726280626
47159CB00023B/2748